RISE OF THE DEMON LORDS

JAMES E WISHER

James E. Wisher

SAND HILL PUBLISHING

The first thing Conryu noticed when he appeared on the Arcane Academy's front lawn was the scent of fresh-mown grass. He smiled and took a deep breath. Living on the floating island, he never bothered with any sort of landscaping. The main building loomed over him, silhouetted by the setting sun. He'd arrived a little early, but not that much. The last thing he wanted was to sit around waiting for the graduation ceremony to begin.

"You're surprised to be here again, Master," said Prime, the floating demon book that was also his familiar. Prime's leather cover had split, revealing a mouth filled with fangs. It looked big enough to bite someone's face off and Conryu had threatened to have him do exactly that on several occasions. It was always amusing to see people's faces when he did.

"Of course. My days of formal classes are long past. Besides, I usually bring trouble along with me and I don't want to cause problems for Dean Blane."

He released the Staff of All Elements and willed it into a pocket dimension that would keep it handy, but out of sight.

Not that he expected any trouble. After saving the Alliance from the survivors of Atlantis, he'd struck a deal with the president. No one would hunt him or try and control him and, in exchange, he agreed to lend a hand should any major magical threat appear. It was basically the same deal Conryu had wanted in the first place, but he didn't point that out. No sense rubbing the man's nose in it.

He turned toward the slightly smaller five-story dorm and set out. The buildings still seemed far too modern for a magic school. He remembered when he first arrived expecting castles and towers only to find modern steel-and-glass buildings. Pretty disappointing, not that he cared anymore. All that mattered now was that he'd get to see Maria, Kelsie, and his mother.

He'd worn his usual uniform of jeans and gray t-shirt. Since he basically hadn't attended any classes during his senior year and few enough his junior year, he hardly thought he'd earned enough credits to graduate. He was here for Maria. She'd worked so hard it would have been an insult to her if he didn't show up.

He jogged up the steps and pushed the front door open. The entry hall was empty though he smelled something delicious cooking in the nearby kitchen. He'd skipped lunch and his mouth watered.

"Conryu!" He turned just in time to catch the petite form of Dean Blane as she leapt into his arms and hugged him. He hadn't even sensed her presence which was a testament to her skill as a wizard. As was her habit, the dean looked like a thirteen-year-old girl in a pale-blue robe with blond pigtails.

He let her hang on for a moment before lowering her to the floor. "Dean Blane. Pretty quiet. I figured there'd be people rushing around not to mention the students' families here to enjoy the festivities."

She shook her head. "The ceremony is for the students and staff. Whatever the families want to do, they can do when everyone gets home tomorrow. You need to get ready. I left a formal robe in your old room. You're welcome to use it until you leave tomorrow."

"Thanks." He hadn't actually planned to stay overnight, but didn't want to be rude. Besides, it might be nice to sleep in his old room one last time.

She waved and hurried off toward the dining hall, probably to oversee the final preparations.

"That is the oddest human I have ever met," Prime said.

"What about Professor McDoogle?" Conryu headed toward the basement stairs.

"I stand corrected: the second oddest."

Conryu grinned and at the bottom of the stairs ducked into his old room. Everything was exactly as he remembered it. Same narrow bed, same chest of drawers, same modest bathroom.

Out of curiosity, he stepped into the bathroom and asked, "Are you here?"

A watery female figure emerged from the shower and smiled at him. He smiled back, delighted to see the naiad again. A wave of nostalgia that surprised him washed over Conryu as he went back to his bedroom and collected the black robe folded neatly on his chest of drawers. When he first arrived, he'd imagined this place as a wizard prison, but now he had only fond thoughts, despite some of the catastrophes that happened during his time here.

Now for the robe. He held it up and frowned. The formal robe had a collar so high it would reach the top of his ears.

Silver runes covered the hem and cuffs. He looked them over but sensed no magic and they didn't mean anything to him.

Prime sniffed. "Simple decorations. They serve no practical purpose."

That wasn't necessarily a bad thing. Conryu had so much magic at his disposal, he hardly needed more. He shrugged and threw the impractical-looking thing over his head. It fit well and the collar didn't even rub anywhere. He conjured a magic mirror and frowned. He looked like an extra in a fantasy movie.

But all things considered, it could have been worse. He'd barely settled on the edge of his bed when Dean Blane's magical voice rang out. "Everyone please join us in the dining hall. It's time for graduation."

He stood back up, relieved not to have to hang around longer than necessary. In the hall, all the senior girls were making their way towards the steps. He spotted Kelsie at once. Her pale face seemed to be floating as it was framed by the dark cloth of her collar and even darker hair. The only color came from her red lipstick that seemed almost unnaturally bright. Unlike the first time they met, her robe fit properly reminding him once again what a beautiful woman she was.

Kelsie smiled at once when she spotted him. They met at the end of the line and hugged.

"It's been too long," she said. "What have you been doing? Wait, let me guess, building bikes and trying to avoid magic?"

He laughed and they started walking behind the others. "Yes to the bikes, but I've made peace with my magic."

"Yes," Prime said, his displeasure plain. "The most powerful wizard in the world and he uses his magic to straighten metal, twist metal, and turn bolts."

"We are not having this debate again," Conryu said.

4

"Fine." Prime closed his mouth, making his cover look like a normal book for the moment.

"I take it your scholomantic still doesn't approve of your hobby?" Kelsie asked.

"It's not a hobby, it's how I make a living. But no, he doesn't. Prime thinks I should take over a small country and proclaim myself wizard king. Why I would want to be a king of any sort is beyond my comprehension."

"Lucky for the world."

They reached the entry hall just as a line of women in white robes reached the bottom floor. He scanned the group until his gaze landed on the stunning figure of Maria Kane. Her long, dark hair spread out over the shoulders of her pure-white robe. Gold markings identical to the ones on his black robe seemed to gleam with an inner light. When Maria's eyes met his she beamed and hurried toward him.

"Don't keep her waiting," Kelsie said. Though their relationship had started out rocky, Maria and Kelsie had become fast friends.

"Thanks."

Conryu met Maria in the center of the hall, picked her up, and swung her around. "I missed you."

When Conryu had set her down she said, "I missed you too. The only good things I can say about the past few months is that nothing tried to kill us and I finished the year at the top of my class."

"Was there ever any doubt?"

"Actually, there was. A couple of the others really came on this year. I only nudged Marisa by a hair."

Conryu glanced around and found they were just about the only ones still in the entry. "We better catch up."

"Yeah. I'm glad you're here. I just wish Mom and Dad could have come too."

He nodded and they walked hand in hand into the dining hall. Conryu's mom was supposed to be around here somewhere, but he hadn't found her yet. She was probably busy working on some project in her workshop and had lost all track of time. His father had died in the chaos of Morgana's invasion of Sentinel City. Just thinking about it still gave him a lump in his throat and probably always would.

Kelsie waved to them from a table on the right-hand side of the room. It looked like everyone was just sitting wherever rather than by element. That suited Conryu as he preferred to stay with Maria. The other girls were comfortable around him now, but he had few really close friends among the group.

At the front of the dining hall, a stage had been set up with a lectern for Dean Blane. He glanced around and quickly spotted Ms. Umbra and the other teachers standing along the back wall behind the stage. He thought about waving, but decided against it. He saw no sign of his mother amongst the group.

Oh well, it wouldn't have been fair to have his mother there when no one else could.

The door to the kitchen opened and Dean Blane came trotting out, a big smile on her face. She went right to the lectern, mumbled a spell, and flew up so her head appeared over the top of it.

"All right, everyone." Her voice carried easily throughout the room, no doubt the result of yet more magic. "Let's get this show on the road."

She called names one after another, starting with the dark magic group. Kelsie went up second, collected a diploma wrapped with a black ribbon, and hurried back to their table.

"Congratulations," Conryu said. "You earned it."

"Second to last in my class." She shook her head. "Not very impressive. Still, Mom doubted I'd pass at all, so it's something."

Dean Blane finished darkness and moved on to fire without calling him up. That came as no surprise to Conryu. He hadn't expected any kind of formal acknowledgement. He was no scholar and everyone knew it.

The light magic group went last and Maria was the final member of the group to get her diploma, this one wrapped in a white ribbon.

He figured that would be it, but Dean Blane went on. "And finally, a very special diploma in the field of saving the world goes to our very own Conryu Koda. Come on up here."

Everyone was looking at him and Maria flashed a huge grin. She knew how much he hated this kind of thing and no doubt found his discomfort amusing. He swallowed a sigh and went up to the stage.

Dean Blane handed him a diploma wrapped with ribbons of every color. "Congratulations."

"Thanks. A degree in saving the world, huh?"

"Seemed appropriate since you've done it twice already." She flew up, hugged him, and kissed his cheek. "Now that the formalities are taken care of, let's eat."

Laden platters came flying out of the kitchen born by invisible spirits. Soft music with no detectable source filled the air. It was pleasant enough and Conryu enjoyed his meal while chatting with the girls about nothing in particular.

When they finished eating, he asked Maria, "So what are your plans after graduation? Still planning to study elf artifacts?"

"I'm not really sure anymore. While researching artifacts is fine, if I find something really dangerous and it ends up in the hands of someone like that general that tried to have you killed, I'm not sure I could live with myself. I definitely want to do some kind of research, but I'm not sure what kind yet."

Conryu hoped she chose something safe. Or at least as safe as anything magical could be.

Out of the corner of his eye he caught Kelsie glancing at him and she quickly looked away. She'd done it a couple times now. He assumed if he had food on his face Maria would have said something.

Speaking of Maria, she leaned in and whispered, "I think she wants to dance."

"Really?"

Conryu wasn't much for dancing, but he could fake it using martial arts footwork if he had to. Not to mention he probably wouldn't see Kelsie for a while after this. So, what the hell. He turned to her and asked, "Would you like to dance?"

Her face lit up. "I'd love to!"

Hand in hand they walked out to an open space and started slow dancing, careful not to get too close and give anyone the wrong idea. Since Maria pointed out what Kelsie was thinking, he figured he wouldn't get in any trouble.

After a minute of silence he asked, "So Maria seems uncertain what she wants to do after graduation. What about you? Even if you're not on good terms with your family, the name should help you find work somewhere."

Her smile twisted. "Grandmother contacted me. She invited me back home and wants me to come help her with a project. Me and my pitiful magic. Maybe since I actually graduated, she's going to ask me to rejoin the family. Anyway, you don't say no to my grandmother, so I have to at least see what she wants."

Kelsie's grandmother was Malice Kincade, the evilest old woman he'd ever met. In fact, Conryu himself had said no to her on more than one occasion, but then he wasn't family and thank heaven for that. If she was doing something with Malice, Kelsie might be in danger.

"Are you sure you don't want a rune coin so you can contact me if you get in trouble?"

"I'm sure. I doubt Mother has given up on adding your bloodline to our family. If you give me one, someone is sure to try and use it to hurt you. I couldn't live with myself if that happened."

She wasn't wrong and after what happened with Jonny during the Atlantis business, getting lured into a trap was at the top of his list of worries. If it kept her safe, he was willing to take the risk. But he wouldn't force her.

The song stopped and he said, "Alright, but be careful. I wouldn't put anything past that hag."

Kelsie's smile returned. "Me either, but she's still family."

"You're a better person than they deserve."

Maria came up and put her hand on his shoulder. "My turn."

Kelsie returned to their table and he and Maria danced to the next tune. She laid her head on his chest and they sort of rocked back and forth more than danced.

"You looked upset," Maria said at last, looking up at him with her dark-brown eyes. "What kind of mess is she in now?"

Conryu told her. "Anything to do with Malice puts me immediately on guard. But like she said, they are family, so all I can do is hope for the best."

He could also arrange for a couple Daughters of the Reaper to keep an eye on Kelsie, just in case. And he intended to, just as soon as he finished up here.

"If she ends up in trouble, you'll be the first one to rush in." Conryu couldn't deny that. Before he could reply, Maria went on. "I don't have to focus on my studies anymore. What do you say I stop by your room once this get-together breaks up?"

His heart raced and when he could finally speak, he said, "Sounds like a great idea."

———

Conryu paced in his room. When he arrived, he'd immediately tossed the fancy robe in the corner out of the way. While it wasn't as uncomfortable as he'd feared when he first saw it, that didn't mean he wanted to wear it a moment longer than necessary. He and Maria parted ways in the entry hall when she said she needed to go upstairs and change. His mind raced around in circles as he imagined what she might change into.

Whatever she chose, he hoped it wouldn't take her long. He'd been waiting years for this moment and the last minutes felt like weeks.

"Kai."

The slender but still feminine figure of his personal body-guard, ninja, and all-around good friend appeared a few feet away. Kai was about six inches shorter than him, dressed in all black from the mask and hood that covered her head to her matching split-toed sandals.

She took a knee and lowered her gaze to the floor. "You called, Chosen."

No matter how many times he told her to relax, she always had a formality bias when he called her. "Please stop kneeling. I assume you know Maria is stopping by soon."

She nodded. Since Kai was always keeping watch over him

from the borderlands of Hell, the only way she could fail to know was if she'd abandoned her post. And short of an order from him or an attack by demons, nothing would make her do that.

"Until I tell you otherwise, I'm going to need you to keep watch in the hall, out of sight of course."

"Understood, Chosen. No one will disturb you two while I live." She vanished into the borderland before he could tell her not to actually kill anyone. Not that he thought she would. Kai had more sense than that.

Conryu just didn't want an audience for what he hoped was going to happen tonight. Oddly, knowing Cerberus was probably watching didn't bother him. Maybe because he thought of the huge three-headed demon dog as more of a pet than a person despite the fact that he was likely smarter than most people.

Speaking of an audience. "Prime, into the top drawer."

He opened the top drawer of his dresser and Prime flew in without complaint. "Thank you for the reprieve, Master. I have no desire to observe your mating habits."

Conryu slammed the drawer shut a bit harder than necessary. Okay, that was everything. The room was as ready as he could make it.

There was a knock and he hurried to the door. His palms were sweaty and he took a moment to dry them off. When he opened it, Maria stood outside. Conryu's jaw nearly hit the floor. She wore an almost-sheer white silk nightgown that clung to her figure in ways he liked very much indeed.

He stepped aside and she came in without a word. The door closed and Conryu took a breath to steady his racing heart. Heaven above she was beautiful.

"I'm sorry I made you wait so long," she said.

Conryu grinned. "The best things in life require patience. You're worth any wait."

When Maria smiled back the tension drained out of him. This night would be perfect, he knew it.

She reached out and when her hand touched his chest she flinched and snatched it back.

"What…" He felt it a moment later. Pain lanced through his arm and spread through his chest and back.

The source was the Reaper's mark on his forearm. Sparks of black lightning arced out of it. Maria backed as far away from him as she could but her expression grew no less pained.

With all his will he tried to suppress the magic, but nothing worked. The Reaper was determined and for all his power, Conryu might as well have been a mouse trying to stop a river.

Maria finally collapsed, overcome by the overwhelming waves of dark magic.

"Kai!" The ninja appeared and he said, "Get her out of here."

Kai hurried over to Maria, scooped her up off the floor with more strength than her slender body should possess, and fled out into the hall.

Seconds later darkness surrounded Conryu.

When it faded he found himself not in the borderlands of Hell, but rather in the center of the Reaper's throne room. A towering figure dressed in a black robe that hid everything save his glowing red eyes and the skeletal hand that clutched a scythe stood on a raised platform directly ahead of him. Behind the Reaper was a throne of bone beside which sat a glass cylinder as tall as Conryu, filled with floating lights like fireflies.

Scores of beautiful women dressed in black stood facing the throne. Black-feathered wings wrapped each of them like a cloak and they kept their gazes lowered.

Furious as he was, Conryu knew nothing he said would matter to his current host. And since he wanted very much to get back to Maria in one piece, he forced himself to keep his cool.

"Your timing sucks."

"My timing, as you so crudely put it, is driven by forces far beyond your meager mortal understanding." The Reaper's cold, emotionless tone made Conryu shiver. Only someone that had never stood in the presence of a being this powerful could consider Conryu really strong.

He forced himself to remain steady. "So, what did you need?"

"I need you to take my place."

2

Kai stood over the pale figure of the Chosen's beloved and debated what she should do. Maria was in no danger now. Her breathing was strong and Kai could already sense many people coming towards them. She could leave now and rejoin Conryu in Hell. Her duty was to protect him, but if the Reaper himself had summoned him, she would be in no position to help even if she went to him now. Much as it pained her to admit it, Conryu so far outclassed her in power that if he couldn't escape on his own, there was no way her presence would make a difference.

Here, at least, she could protect the one he cared most about. If she was safe, he would be free to focus on whatever situation he found himself in. So you could argue that by remaining with Maria, she was keeping her charge safe.

Smiling a fraction under her black mask at the mental gymnastics she just performed, Kai darted into the now-empty dorm room and retrieved the formal robe Conryu had discarded. She used it to cover Maria and her rather immodest nightgown. She couldn't deny the unconscious woman's beauty. Certainly, it was easy to see why Conryu loved her so much. Though having been with them for several years now, she understood that it was far more than looks that kept the two of them together.

Footsteps on the stairs heralded the arrival of the rescue party. Dean Blane was in the lead with Ms. Umbra and Conryu's mother not far behind. Other teachers brought up the rear along with students, including the other dark aligned that approached from the opposite direction.

"What in the world happened down here?" Dean Blane asked.

Kai bowed to her and said, "The Chosen has been summoned by our master. Maria was rendered unconscious by the surge of dark energy. I believe she has sustained no permanent damage."

Dean Blane knelt beside Maria and passed a hand over her while muttering. "I detect no physical damage. Probably the shock knocked her out."

"Where exactly is my son now?" Mrs. Koda asked.

"In Hell meeting with the Reaper. Before you ask, I have no idea why. The master does not confide such things in servants like me." Mrs. Koda looked especially pale, so Kai added, "I don't believe he means Conryu any harm. Had he wished it, the Reaper could have easily killed him via the link that connects them."

Mrs. Koda's smile held no humor. "You're not very good at reassuring people, are you, dear? Oh, why didn't I leave that stupid project and come to see him graduate?"

Dean Blane stood and patted her hand. "I'm sure he'll be fine. Conryu visits Hell all the time."

"Just to be sure," Ms. Umbra said. "I'll ask my contacts to look into it."

"I don't think there's anything more to be learned here," Dean Blane said. "Let's take Maria up to her room. Off to bed, everyone. Students are going home in the morning. Teachers, if we learn anything, an announcement will be made."

Kai picked Maria up and followed the dean up five flights of stairs and down a modestly long hall to an empty room. Even with magic enhancing her strength it was a haul. "Didn't she have a roommate?"

"One of the other seniors left early so she moved to the empty room," Dean Blane said. "Maria has been on her own for about a month. Lay her on the bed."

Kai did so and they all stood in a circle staring down at the unconscious woman. If she woke up now, she'd probably have a heart attack seeing them all there.

Mrs. Koda looked all around at everything and everyone before finally asking, "What could the Reaper want with my son? I know they have some kind of connection, but I thought Conryu was supposed to be his agent on earth. Dragging him to Hell seems to defeat the purpose."

"Conryu is the most favored servant of the Reaper on earth," Kai said. "Our master may have wished to discuss something with him in person. Even magical communication can be listened in on if a wizard has skill enough. In the Reaper's realm, he can be certain no one will eavesdrop."

Everything Kai said was true, but she said it more to reassure Conryu's mother than because she thought it was the truth. Personally, she figured Conryu was about to be sent on a quest both dangerous and of unbelievable importance. And when the time came for him to depart, Kai would be with him no matter what.

"Guessing is a waste of time," Dean Blane said. "Either

Conryu will let us know himself, or Angeline's agent will find out. Until then, we'll have to be patient."

Kai was trained as an assassin. She could sit still and keep watch with the best of them. But when the person she was charged with protecting was alone and in danger and there was nothing she could do to help, waiting became a maddening experience.

A tingle ran through Kai and she reached for her sword.

"What—" Dean Blane's question was cut off when a circle of black flames appeared in the air above them.

Conryu's face filled the space a moment later. Kai relaxed and swallowed a sigh of relief. He appeared unharmed.

"I hope I didn't worry you all too much." His gaze shifted to the still-unconscious Maria. "Is she okay?"

"As far as I can tell," Dean Blane said. "What's going on?"

"I don't have all the details yet. But for the foreseeable future, I'm going to be filling in for the Reaper. You're looking at the new ruler of Hell."

Dean Blane and Mrs. Koda stared, seeming unable to speak. Even Kai's mouth was partway open under her mask. She couldn't remember anything like this happening before.

"I'm sure you all have questions. Once I get a better handle on what's going on, I'll be in touch. I just wanted to let you know I was safe and to check on Maria. I'm trusting you to keep her safe, Kai."

Kai knelt and bowed her head. "My life for hers, Chosen."

"That's what I wanted to hear. If you need help, don't hesitate to call in reinforcements. I have to go. You-know-who is getting impatient. Talk again soon." The circle of flames vanished.

Dean Blane shook her head. "How does that boy get himself into these messes?"

Mrs. Kane appeared on the verge of hyperventilating. Kai knew how she felt. Instead of being Chosen, Conryu was about to actually become the Reaper. And he trusted her to protect the one he loved the most.

It was an honor beyond anything she could have imagined.

———

"If you're finished with your call." The Reaper's cold voice dragged Conryu back to the moment. He'd been so relieved when Dean Blane said there was nothing wrong with Maria that he'd actually forgotten for a moment the situation he was in.

"Right, thank you for that. What exactly do you want me to do?"

"Sit on my throne and try to relax, that will reduce the discomfort a little. I will do the rest. Don't worry, this won't kill you. In fact, you are about to become as close to a god as a mortal will ever be."

Conryu didn't especially like being a wizard. Upgrading to god didn't appeal to him either. But he didn't seem to have much choice and it was only temporary.

Not wanting to test his host's patience any further, he climbed the steps to the bone throne and sat. A chill ran up his spine and if he'd had longer hair it would have been standing on end. The Reaper moved behind the throne and rested his bony fingers on Conryu's shoulders. Prime hovered a few feet away, for once keeping his mouth shut.

Was this what it felt like right before you died? Conryu wouldn't have doubted it for a second. It felt like his soul had turned to ice.

A moment later his blood turned to flames as power unlike

anything he'd ever imagined poured into him. It made the Reaper taking over his body during the incident with Morgana feel like nothing.

The process seemed to last forever. When the pain subsided, he didn't actually feel any different. At some point the Reaper had removed his fingers from Conryu's shoulders. The giant black form loomed silently behind him, still as a statue.

He waved a hand in front of the Reaper's shadowy cowl. "Hello?"

"His mind has gone to meet with the other eight lords of hell." One of the black-winged angels stepped away from her sisters. Conryu recognized Narumi at once. She'd been Kai's teacher before getting killed and reborn in her current form, that of a beautiful fallen angel. During the Atlantis incident, they'd met briefly before Kai said her goodbye.

"Narumi, it's good to see you again. I assume you're the one who's going to instruct me on what I'm supposed to do now?"

"I'm pleased you remember me, Chosen. And yes, our master selected me to serve as your guide while you're filling in for him. There is much you need to know and many preparations that must be made should Lord Null fail in his efforts to convince the other eight to stay out of matters on your earth."

Conryu was already getting a headache. Why couldn't Maria have been Chosen? She loved this stuff.

"I, of course, will be lending my considerable knowledge to the task as well. Now that the restrictions have been removed, I will be free to instruct you properly." Prime couldn't have sounded more pompous if he tried.

"Let's start with who the other eight are and what you meant about my earth."

"The eight are the rulers of the other hells. Each is as powerful as the Reaper and as different as a squirrel is from a rat. As for your earth, there are multiple earths, one in each galaxy to be precise, with exactly the same land masses, the same amount of water, and the same sun. Each has a human population. That is where the similarities end as each has developed in its own way and at its own pace. Controlling one is a great prize among the nine lords of hell."

His headache wasn't getting any better. "Okay, if there are eight other hells, why do I always end up in this one when I open a gate?"

Prime jumped in. "For the past five thousand years, our master has controlled access to your earth. He won the right in one of the nine's endless contests. Any spell cast on your earth that involves demons or dark magic draws on this hell. Were you to visit another world, the magic you've been taught wouldn't work. Too many hells to choose from."

"Five thousand years ago." Conryu ran a hand through his hair. "That was about the time Lemuria was founded and our modern system of magic created, right?"

Narumi smiled. "Right. Your earth is an experiment, Chosen. The Reaper, the archangel you know as the Goddess, and the rulers of the four elemental realms struck a grand bargain. They agreed to work together, at least as much as their nature allows, to create a new form of magic that they would teach to mortals. Thus was the elemental school of wizardry born. As you've seen, it's become highly successful."

"Sure, when you kill off anyone with a different style of magic, it tends to make yours more popular. Let's get down to the bottom line. When the deal the Reaper made with his fellow demon lords is up, will our magic still work?"

"Most of it will. Dark magic users will need to modify their spells to specify which hell they wish to call upon, but that is a simple matter for a skilled wizard. Your own magic won't be affected since you're connected directly to our master. I doubt you could call upon the magic of another hell if you wanted to."

"That doesn't sound so bad." Conryu stood and walked around on the dais. "Yet I sensed a lot of tension from the Reaper. What am I missing?"

"If the deal ends," Narumi said, "the other lords will start making deals with people on your earth. Sell your soul, get power. How many evil people, men and women, will take that offer? Imagine criminal gangs only instead of mortal weapons and magical artifacts, they have the gift of hellfire or the ability to create undead or any other power you can imagine. The other lords won't limit themselves to a single Chosen. They will give power to anyone willing to trade their soul. Imagine the chaos."

Conryu could easily imagine it. Bad as the fanatics that tried to kill him were, if they'd had access to the sort of powers Narumi described, they would have been ten times worse.

"What can I do? How long do we have?" he asked.

"The pact will end in one earth day. As for what you can do, prepare. I will provide you with all the information we have on the other lords. Share it with your friends. Lord Null has little hope that he will succeed. You must be ready to fight the threat when it arrives."

"But time stops while I'm here, so I have all the time in the world, right?"

"No. The flow of time is controlled by the perceptions of the lord. Since that's you, time will flow here exactly as it does on earth."

So much for that advantage.

"I didn't know that," Prime said. Conryu was surprised the scholomantic would admit such a thing.

Conryu scowled and massaged his temples in hopes of warding off another headache. He might not fully understand everything that was going on, but he knew it would be bad.

Still, he'd never shied away from a fight and he wouldn't shy away from this one. If anyone tried to ruin his world, he'd kick their ass.

3

The first thing Maria noticed as she came slowly awake was the lack of pain. That last wave of dark magic felt like it lit every nerve in her body on fire. She opened her eyes expecting to find Conryu hovering like a worried mother. Instead she found herself surrounded by Kai, Dean Blane, and Conryu's worried mother. Seeing Mrs. Koda reminded Maria of what they'd been planning to do and what she was wearing.

Her cheeks warmed and she looked down at herself. Happily, someone had covered her with a blanket which hopefully meant only Conryu had seen the special nightgown she'd bought in anticipation of tonight.

So much for that brilliant plan. It seemed something always got in the way. If she'd believed in fate, she might have taken the hint and tried to find a new boyfriend. Not that she could imagine loving anyone as much as she did Conryu.

"Are you feeling okay?" Dean Blane asked. "I didn't find any damage. The surge of dark magic likely overloaded your system and knocked you unconscious."

"I'm fine now. Where's Conryu?"

"In Hell," Kai said. "Our master summoned him. That's what knocked you out. He's been given the honor of filling in for the Reaper."

Maria stared for a moment, her brain failing to process what Kai just said. "What? How? Why?"

"My reaction exactly," Mrs. Koda said. "It never ceases to amaze me the trouble he finds."

"He is Chosen," Kai said as if that explained everything.

The hint of worship in her voice when she spoke to or about Conryu always made Maria wonder if there wasn't more between them than she claimed. Not that she believed Conryu would cheat on her. He wasn't that sort of man. But in her own way, Maria suspected Kai loved Conryu as much as she did.

A tingle ran up Maria's spine and for a moment she feared some dark magic attack. It faded as quickly as it appeared and when it did, a circle of black flames appeared with Conryu's face in the middle.

He looked right at her and showed her the smile that always melted her heart. "I'm glad you're okay."

"I'm glad *you're* okay," she said. "Now what's this craziness about you taking over for the Reaper?"

"Kind of a long story and I'm afraid it's not going to have a happy ending."

Conryu told them of the other hells and other Earths. If it was anyone else, she would have assumed they'd escaped from a mental asylum. Given who and where he was, she had no doubt everything Conryu said was the truth. Frankly, she would have preferred if he'd gone mad.

"I can't return until the Reaper finishes his meeting and reclaims his post. I'm hoping you guys can help me out with the preparations. I'll let Lord Talon know as well as the Daughters of the Reaper. Once that's done, I'm going to focus on learning as much as I can here."

"I'll alert the dark magic users as well as the government," Dean Blane said. "Sounds like we have little time to alter the spells so they'll work when our new situation begins."

"Don't let the president give you any shit," Conryu said. "All the governments need to know what's coming, even the ones he doesn't like."

"Ha! If he doesn't tell them, I'll do it myself."

Conryu nodded, then turned to Maria and her chest tightened. She really wasn't cut out for nonstop world-threatening problems. "I hate to ask again, but could you do some research for me?"

She immediately let out a breath she hadn't realized she was holding. She could do research, no sweat. "Sure, what do you need to know?"

"Anything you can find about ancient temples from at least five thousand years ago. The lords might have used different names, but there should be some hints about their true identities. Whatever you find will be great."

"I'll get started first thing in the morning. Oh, but we're supposed to leave in the morning."

Dean Blane waved a hand. "Under the circumstances, you're welcome to stay and use the library as long as you need to. Don't give it a thought."

"What about me?" Mrs. Koda asked.

Conryu chewed his lip and finally said, "I'm not sure, Mom. If there's anything you've been working on that will be useful against dark magic, I'm sure it will come in handy. Until we figure out more about how the other lords' magic works, I'm not even sure myself what needs to be done."

"That's okay, dear. Whatever you need, whenever you need it, give me the word."

"Thanks, Mom. I've got to go, but should we plan to get together again in, say, forty-eight hours?"

"Sounds good," Dean Blane said. "Next time we'll meet up in the library."

Conryu nodded. "Good luck everyone."

He vanished, leaving Maria and the others alone. She turned to Dean Blane. "Did you have any idea there were other hells and demon lords like the Reaper?"

"I've heard ancient legends about monsters and evil magic. Pretty much every society has them. Now I can't help wondering how many of those old stories are more than fairy tales."

Maria had a sinking feeling they were all going to find out far sooner than they'd like.

———

Conryu blew out a long sigh of relief. Maria appeared fully recovered, thank goodness. Dean Blane said she'd be okay, but seeing her up, awake, and aware took a load off his mind. Not that he didn't have plenty of other things to think about.

He'd moved to a small antechamber off the throne room to make his call. It really wasn't much more than an empty square room with two doors, one leading to a hall outside and another to the throne room. If he was anywhere else, he would have called it a coat room.

Outside, the black-winged angels were breaking up and soon only Narumi and the honor guard would remain. He still preferred to manage things without an audience.

Fewer people to laugh when he screwed up.

Now he needed to talk to Kanna. After he explained everything, she could pass it on to Lord Talon. Conryu didn't want to have this conversation more than twice.

Given his new power set, calling her should be easy enough. He pictured the beautiful ninja and said, "Kanna."

The summons rippled across Hell and a moment later she appeared in front of him on one knee. "Master?"

"Guess again."

She looked up and her dark eyes were wide. "Chosen? Why did your call feel like it came from the Reaper?"

"I'll give you the short version." When he finished Conryu said, "From the sounds of it, things are going to get bad back home. I'll need to call on you and the others more than usual."

"Please don't speak as if you fear to burden us. Our lives have been yours since the moment the master chose you as his representative on earth. We shed our blood or the blood of your enemies with equal willingness. Give me your orders."

Conryu swallowed a sigh. It was good to have them on his side, but he had to be ever so careful with his commands as they would throw themselves into certain death should he wish it.

"Okay, I've got Kai keeping an eye on Maria, but she might need help. Could you arrange some backup for her?"

"I'll send a squad and should Kai need more, she need only ask."

"Good. Next, I want you to send someone to keep an eye on Kelsie. I don't trust her grandmother as far as I can throw the old bat. Finally, I need you to fill Lord Talon in on the situation. If I think of anything else I'll be in touch."

"Very well, Chosen."

Kanna stared at him and Conryu finally realized he'd

brought her here using his power. On her own, she'd have to fly back to the borderland before she returned.

He reached out and placed a hand on Kanna's chest just below her throat. Power flowed into her, drawing a gasp.

"There, that should be enough of a boost to let you travel directly between the mortal world and Black City. I don't know if it will last once I lose the Reaper's power, but for now it should make things easier for us both. Off you go."

She bowed and vanished.

He finally let out the sigh he'd been holding in. Now it was time to go to demon class. He could hardly contain his excitement.

4

As the train slowed for the approach to Central City's station, Kelsie felt herself tensing up. She hadn't been home in nearly three years. What kind of welcome should she expect? She nearly laughed. Not a warm one, that was certain.

No doubt Dean Blane warning them all about the change to dark magic that should go into effect in the next few hours wasn't helping.

At least Ms. Umbra had told them what they needed to do to make their spells work normally. Kelsie wasn't a fast caster at the best of times and having to remember to alter her spells to include the Reaper's name in Infernal at the end of each incantation would slow her down even more. Even worse, this was only a theory. Until someone tested every dark magic spell to make sure it worked correctly, they wouldn't really know for sure.

She shifted in the buttery soft leather chair. One of the few good things about traveling as an official Kincade was the travel arrangements. They always had a private suite on the train and should she have to fly, it would certainly be on one of the family's planes. Though she couldn't deny wishing she was strong enough to travel through Hell the way Conryu did, this wasn't so bad.

A sigh escaped her when she thought about her dear friend. Maria had found her before she left this morning and told her more details on what he was doing. There were certainly some details left out, no doubt things she didn't want Kelsie's family learning, but what she did say was astonishing. How could a mortal man, even one as powerful as Conryu, fill in for the Reaper?

Kelsie shook her head, more than a little relieved that it wasn't her job to figure this stuff out. Dealing with her family would be more than enough to manage and she already felt a little underwater.

The train lurched slightly then came to a full stop. Forcing herself not to sigh again, she stood and collected her two bags. They were both Kincade Carryalls, magic bags that never weighed more than a few pounds no matter how much you put in them, so she had no trouble handling them both. Her private suite was in the last car and when she stepped out onto the landing everyone had already started making their way toward the turnstiles.

A driver she didn't recognize beyond his Kincade uniform stood on the other side, a sign with her name on it clutched in his hands. Nearly six and a half feet tall and dressed in all black, he towered over most of the other people gathered to pick up their loved ones. She hadn't expected one of the family to meet her, but couldn't they at least have sent someone she knew to pick her up? It wasn't a good start to her return home.

What she wouldn't have given to have Maria and Conryu here with her.

On the other side of the turnstiles, her driver held out his hands for the bags. "Welcome back, Miss."

"Thank you." His deep, calm voice salved her nerves. "Are we going home or to the corporate building?"

"The mansion. Your grandmother has been working from home for the last several weeks." He leaned down and lowered his voice. "The pains have grown worse and her temper is shorter than ever. Your mother has taken to sleeping at the office to avoid her."

Kelsie winced. That was worse than she feared. "We'd best not keep her waiting then."

"No, Miss."

The crowd parted around her driver and soon they were in the limo. It was a black, Kincade custom design with bullet-proof glass, armored doors, and wards against magic. The thing was virtually a tank and for all she knew it might have a cannon in there somewhere.

The driver insisted she sit in the back and she didn't argue. Any time she tried to be friendly with the servants they balked. Family and servants didn't fraternize, it was an ironclad household rule. Kelsie hated it since she liked the servants better than most of her relatives. Not that she would ever do anything to get someone fired just to make herself feel better.

The streets were packed with honking cars. Pedestrians with no concern for their wellbeing darted across the street drawing yet more honks. Fortunately, they only had to pass through a modest section of the city and then they were in the outskirts. Everything calmed instantly. Everything except Kelsie. When the streets grew quiet, she knew they were close to home.

Sure enough, five minutes later they reached the gate to the mansion. The driver pressed a button on the dash and the gate slid aside so they could make the long drive up to the main house. The grounds were perfectly manicured, a situation made possible by a small army of landscapers. They probably could have taken care of it with magic, but there was a certain pride that came with maintaining a proper staff. Basically, it made her mother feel like more of a big shot.

They parked in front of the front door. Standing at the top of the steps was the head butler. The old man in his black uniform, a tuft of white hair circling his bald head, looked like a vulture waiting to pick her bones clean.

She shuddered and climbed out of the limo. The driver walked up the steps behind her and set her bags on the landing. Couldn't have the outside servants setting foot in the house, heaven forbid.

"Welcome home, Miss." The butler gave her a little bow. "Your grandmother gave instructions for you to be brought to her office as soon as you arrived. If you'll follow me."

He phrased it as a request, but Kelsie recognized an order when she heard one. She also knew there was no point in fighting it. The sooner she dealt with her grandmother, the sooner she could try and figure out her real future. Four years at the Arcane Academy had done little to help her make up her mind.

The abstract paintings from her last visit had been swapped out for landscapes. That must have been the fashion of the season. She assumed Mother kept someone on staff to keep track of such stupid things. They looked every bit as expensive as the old paintings.

She shook her head and followed the butler to the right-hand-most section of the wing. Grandmother preferred to work as far from the living area as possible. They came to a closed oak door and the butler knocked.

A muffled grunt came from inside followed by her grandmother's sour voice. "Send her in."

The door opened and the butler stepped aside with a knowing look. She swallowed her third sigh and walked into the wood-paneled room. Bookshelves held hundreds of books of magic. Her grandmother sat behind a cherry desk, its surface covered with papers and a telephone on the right corner. The wrinkles had deepened around her eyes and mouth, but her eyes were brighter and more determined than Kelsie had ever seen.

"Hello, Grandmother," Kelsie said.

"Sit, girl. I assume you heard about the dark magic?"

"Dean Blane told us this morning. Have you tested the workaround?"

Her grandmother glanced at the clock ticking away on the wall. "According to my calculations we still have one hour before the change. As soon as it happens, every dark magic aligned wizard in the government will begin testing. It won't take long to work out if the boy's warning amounts to anything. Personally, I hope he's playing the most elaborate prank in history. I have too much to do for this to interfere."

"Conryu wouldn't do that."

"I know, but an old woman can hope, can't she?" Grandmother pinched her nose with a gnarled hand. "Anyway, the government is in a panic. Half of them are trying to figure out who we can take advantage of during this crisis and the other half are trying to avoid us getting taken advantage of. My explanation, that no one is going to be doing anything until matters settle, fell on deaf ears. So I've got idiots from every department calling constantly. Even worse, my contact says she needs more time to make sure the process will still work.

Days, weeks, months, I don't know. Hopefully not months. I'm not certain I have that long."

Hearing her grandmother state straight out that she only had weeks to live shocked Kelsie to the core. While there had never been much warmth in their relationship, Grandmother had been a steady presence in her life forever.

"Won't you tell me what this is all about? Other than having me accompany you somewhere, to do something, with someone, I have no idea what's really happening. Maybe I can help."

Grandmother shook her head. "You're too weak to be of any use. I want you along in case something goes wrong. That boy is clearly fond of you. If you're in danger, he'll come rescue you and hopefully me in the process. Other than that, you're baggage. Return to your room, rest, and prepare. As soon as I get word from my contact, we're leaving."

Kelsie stood and stalked out. So much for her hope of a fresh start with her family.

Any pity she'd felt for Malice was long gone. She didn't bother pointing out that Conryu was bound in Hell and that he couldn't come to the rescue if he wanted to. And even if he wasn't, she had no way to contact him. Her grandmother obviously wasn't thinking clearly.

If that was the case, Kelsie would have to be doubly on guard.

5

The worst day of Miguel's life was rapidly turning into the worst night. Waves lapped against the side of his modest fishing boat. The nets sat empty on the floor. He'd spent hours trawling his usual spot and nothing, no snapper, no grouper, no nothing. It felt like the fish had all picked up and moved as one. Nothing had happened in the area as far as he knew. In fact, he'd made a good catch only two days earlier in the same spot.

But if he wanted to eat, he needed to catch, so he revved up his little outboard and set out for new water. That was eight hours ago, before the squall that came up out of nowhere. The winds had howled and he feared his boat might get swamped. Then his motor died leaving him at the mercy of the wind and current. With no other options he held on for dear life and prayed that he would survive.

And so he did, but now he had no idea where he was or how to find his way back home. Hopefully once the sun fully set the clouds would part and reveal the stars. Unfortunately, without a motor, he'd have a long paddle home.

The only good thing about night falling was it took the worst of the heat away. The sun beating down on him left his already leathery skin scorched and cracked. Sometimes when he looked in the mirror, he saw not a twenty-five-year-old man, but his father, worn down by a lifetime of hard work on the sea. Wish as he might for a different life, Miguel was stuck and fishing was the only legal way to earn his keep.

Miguel sighed and took a sip of his rapidly dwindling water. Some days it didn't pay to roll out of the hammock.

The front of the ship bumped into something, jarring him out of his half doze. Scrambling up for a closer look, he leaned over the rail. A rock barely jutted out of the water. Lucky for him the boat had been going slowly enough that it did no damage.

Looking up from the water his eyes widened.

An island!

And not so far away. With a silent thank-you to whichever guardian angel had nudged his boat this way, he dug out his oar and started paddling.

An hour of effort brought him burning shoulders and a soft landing on a sandy beach. Leaping out, he dragged the boat above the high tide mark. Exhausted, he collected his water jug and gutting knife before trudging up to the edge of the jungle. He sprawled out on the sand under a palm tree and was soon fast asleep.

It seemed no time had passed when he sat bolt upright. He had a nightmare, a horrible one, unlike anything he'd ever dreamed. So real it might have been a memory.

The moon had fully risen and by its dim light he saw four hunched-over figures pawing at his boat. They walked on two legs, but had arms so long they nearly touched the ground. If they damaged his boat he'd never get out of here.

He raised a hand.

Stay silent!

The voice in his head shocked him so that he couldn't have spoken if he wanted to. Was he going mad? First the dream, then those creatures, now a voice in his head. Perhaps he was really unconscious out on the water waiting to die.

You're not going mad and you're not on the water. Though if you ignore me, you may well end up dead. You've landed on the island of a necromancer. Those creatures are her minions and it's only a matter of time before they sense your presence. I've hidden you for the time being, but that can't last.

Miguel's life really had gone to hell. Everyone knew about the cursed island and stayed well away. The storm must have blown him further off course than he'd thought. Escaping by boat was impossible with those things in the way.

He glanced at the jungle. Given his options, that was the only way, but he might run into more of the creatures in the dark.

What was he supposed to do?

I can guide you to a sanctuary. But you have to trust me and do exactly as I say.

What choice did he have?

None. Stand up slowly. Make no sound.

Slowly and painfully, Miguel eased himself to his feet. Every second he expected the four monsters to turn his way. But nothing happened. Maybe the owner of the mysterious voice was a guardian angel. Though hopefully not the same one that brought him to this island.

Fifteen feet to your right is a path leading into the jungle. Follow it. Quietly.

Miguel spotted the gap in the trees and tiptoed to it. He walked slowly, too slowly given what lurked behind him.

When he looked back and could no longer see the creatures, he let out a long breath.

Something howled in the dark.

Idiot! They've got your scent now.

"You said to be quiet, not hold my breath. What do I do?"

Run and open your mind to me. I will guide your course.

Miguel wasn't sure how to do that, but he ran and tried not to think, mostly about the things he heard crashing through the forest behind him.

He made a sharp right, down a path he hadn't even seen. Miguel had never met a wizard, but this had to be magic.

Maybe the necromancer was guiding him into a trap.

He dismissed the idea at once. If the voice belonged to the master of this island, she would have simply let her monsters have him.

Another gap appeared and he darted down it before fully registering what he was doing.

The crashing grew louder by the second.

Wherever the sanctuary the voice promised waited, he'd best get there soon.

Lucky for him, soon turned out to be fifteen strides later. He stopped in front of a vine-covered ruin. The stone building had been partially claimed by the jungle, but still looked sound. The problem was, there appeared to be no way in.

A grinding sound filled the air as a section of the wall sank into the ground.

With the roars of the monsters loud in his ears, Miguel slipped through the opening. The door sealed back up behind him, leaving him in absolute darkness. A chill ran through him despite the heat and humidity. He wasn't sure his situation had improved much, but at least he was alive.

"What now?" he asked, in the hope that the voice that guided him here hadn't abandoned him.

Now it is time for us to meet. You have entered my temple. Follow the light to the altar chamber and we will discuss your future.

The only future that interested Miguel was one that saw him far from this island and its monsters. If he could manage a boat full of fish, that would be a nice bonus.

A glowing green ball appeared in front of him. It cast strange, wavering shadows over the crumbling walls. When it started deeper into the building, Miguel followed. The owner of the voice had saved his life after all, it would have been rude not to at least hear him out. Besides, there was no other way out.

The light bobbed slowly along, giving him plenty of time to examine his surroundings. The initial entryway quickly widened into a collection of larger chambers, each painted with murals depicting various activities. In one, people offered clay jars to an altar, in another a large group knelt in front of what he assumed was this temple and prayed. Miguel didn't look too closely at the images that showed figures being cut open on the same altar.

In his history class as a child, he learned about things like this happening in ancient times. If this temple was that old, then some magic must have preserved these paintings. They appeared nearly as vibrant as the day they were made.

He swallowed the lump in his throat. Exactly what sort of being had he stumbled across?

The light led him into the largest room so far. He stopped just inside the entrance to stare. It had a high, vaulted ceiling that disappeared into the darkness above. On a raised dais at the rear sat a golden altar covered in a black cloth embroidered with a jagged red symbol Miguel had never seen before. His guide stopped and floated directly above the altar, almost in invitation.

Miguel debated his options, but only for a second. Really, they came down to trusting the one that saved him or taking his chances with the monsters outside, assuming he could even open the door on his own.

Steeling himself, he strode across the room and stopped in front of the altar. "What happens now?"

Vines rose out of cracks in the floor, twisting and wrapping around themselves until a humanoid figure stood in front of him. Its eyes glowed with the same green as the light that led him here.

"Now we talk for real." Though it had no mouth, the figure spoke with the same voice as the one that appeared in his head. "My name is Baphomet and this is my temple. For long years I have been gone from the earth, but now my time of banishment is at an end."

"Congratulations?" Miguel had never heard the name Baphomet but didn't want to insult the obviously powerful creature.

"Thank you. And your ignorance does not insult me. I have been gone for five thousand years. There is no reason you would recognize my name. That is something I will change. I hope with your assistance."

Miguel tried to imagine how he could assist this being and failed to come up with anything.

"I require an agent in this world. I can only project myself to my temples, of which this is one of only a handful remaining. As my chosen agent, you will gain great power, but you will also have the responsibility to extend my reach across the whole world. My enemies will try and stop you. You will need to be strong and brave. I sense those are qualities you already possess."

Miguel didn't consider himself either especially brave or strong. Going out on the ocean to fish took some courage, but many men did the same thing.

"I appreciate you saving me, truly, but I'm just a fisherman. Perhaps someone wiser would better suit your needs."

"No, you will suit my needs perfectly. Have you not always desired more than your modest lot in life? Join me and you will know true power. The sort of power that will make men tremble at your approach. You've seen men like that. And you envy them even as you hate them. I can see it all in your mind."

Miguel winced. It was true. When the drug dealers with their fancy clothes and rolls of money came to the island looking for desperate fishermen to run their drugs north, he did envy them that power. He hated himself for that, but couldn't deny the appeal.

"Serve me and you will have power enough to make those men prostrate themselves before you. What say you, Miguel? Will you become my Chosen on earth?"

Miguel took a deep breath. Heaven help him. "I will."

"Excellent choice." A foot-long piece of needle-sharp wood grew up out of the altar. "Take the thorn, pierce your hand, and let your blood drip on the altar."

Miguel grimaced and picked up the thorn. It weighed more than he expected, more like steel than wood. He barely touched it to his palm and it sliced right through.

Blood dripped on the black cloth and was instantly absorbed. Miguel felt the link between him and Baphomet strengthen into something far stronger than chains. It felt like they shared a soul.

"We do," the vine man said. "With your blood offering, your

soul is now mine. Serve me well and in death you shall know even greater power in Hell."

That didn't sound so great, but he'd made his choice. "So what do I do now?"

"Now you need instruction on how to wield your new power. Prepare yourself for the exchange of information."

"How—" His question was cut off when the vine man broke apart and reached for him. Hundreds of vines wrapped him like a mummy from head to toe. The rich scent of loam and blood filled his nostrils and along with it the knowledge of what he could now do.

His mind reeled, unable to fully comprehend this new knowledge. Assuming Baphomet wasn't lying, he was now stronger than any wizard. He might be the strongest being in the world.

He didn't know how much time passed, but finally the vines released him and he fell to his knees in front of the altar. His torn, canvas clothes were gone, replaced by fine black robes embroidered with the same red symbol as the one on the altar covering.

When he lifted his gaze, he found the covering gone. That answered the question of where the cloth came from.

Now you have power and the knowledge of how to use it. Your first task is to eliminate the squatter that has dared to make my island her home.

Kill the necromancer? It seemed his new master didn't plan to ease him into his new duties.

6

The Reaper's library was every bit as big as Conryu had imagined. Having an eternity to collect information, from what he'd been told was billions upon billions of worlds, led to a massive heap of books. He wished Maria could have seen it. She'd have gone nuts. Unfortunately, since it was in Hell, she also would have died instantly, so a visit was out of the question.

At the table beside him, Narumi was droning on about the cosmic entities known as the Creator and the Destroyer. Apparently, one made universes and the other smashed them to nothingness. Then after this universe was made, the Creator decided he liked it too well and tried to stop the Destroyer. When they touched, they exploded. The remains of the Creator became the race of angels and the remains of the Destroyer became the race of demons. Where their blood mingled, the race of true dragons was born.

While the demons were busy fighting and consuming each other, the angels worked together to forge a prison for them. The prison became the nine hells and all the demons absorbed each other until only the nine lords of hell remained, omnipotent beings trapped in an inescapable prison. Every other demon was created by them, one way or another.

Prime felt the need to chime in every now and then, even though he had little to add to Narumi's lecture. It was as if the scholomantic couldn't stand the idea of anyone else teaching him something. Who'd have ever imagined a demon book with a fragile ego?

"Are you listening?" Narumi asked.

"I got the gist. How come the Reaper doesn't set up a server system, digitize all these books, and make searchable files? That would be so much easier."

Narumi rubbed her smooth, perfect face with an equally perfect hand. Though she'd been in her sixties when she died, she was reborn as a black-winged angel in her prime. "Not every world, in fact not even most worlds, have advanced technology. But everyone understands books. That makes it easy for anyone visiting from any world to access the information they seek."

"Oh, right. I'm still not used to the idea of more worlds where humans live. We knew about the elves that invaded hundreds of years ago, so I guess it shouldn't have been that big of a surprise."

"Those invaders weren't true elves," Prime said. He was getting ready to launch into another lecture, Conryu could see it in his eyes. "They were a near-human species that happened to share some physical characteristics that you associate with elves. In reality—"

The door to the library burst open and another beautiful black-winged angel hurried in. She looked as anxious as he'd ever seen one of the former ninjas get. Her dark eyes were wide and her wings twitched as if she'd lost control of them.

"Forgive the interruption, Chosen, but Lucifer has appeared in the palace and demands that you come to the throne room at once to speak with him."

Conryu grimaced. If there was one thing he wanted to do less than learn about the true nature of elves, it was talk to Lucifer.

"I have all the Reaper's power, right? How bad would it be if I turned Lucifer into a hamster and tossed him in a cage?"

"The cage part would be fine," Narumi said. "The hamster part would be a problem. Lucifer oversees a number of cults on many worlds and if he were transformed into an animal incapable of rational thought, many of our master's schemes would be put in jeopardy."

"Fine. So I can put him in a cage, but no hamster. Pity, but whatever. Let's go see what he wants."

Conryu pushed away from the table and Narumi joined him with Prime floating a safe distance behind them. He took a step toward the door then frowned. Why was he walking?

With a thought the room shifted and he was standing in the center of the throne room. He grinned but the expression withered when he looked up and found Lucifer sitting on the throne. His very human face was almost painfully handsome and the crimson-skinned torso below perfectly muscled. It even looked like he'd combed the hair of his goat legs. A black trident leaned against the throne in easy reach.

Twenty black-winged angels that served as throne room guards surrounded him, their hands near the hilts jutting up beside their heads. They all looked tense, as if expecting a fight. Clearly they didn't appreciate Lucifer claiming his seat any more than Conryu did.

"You're in my chair," Conryu said.

"This isn't your chair, little human, it's his." Lucifer jerked a thumb over his shoulder at the Reaper's still form.

"Well, until he gets back, it's mine. Now bounce."

Lucifer crossed his legs and made no effort to get up.

All Conryu's anger and frustration came bubbling up. "Move!"

The full weight of his limitless power lifted Lucifer up off the throne and hurled him toward the ceiling like a rocket. He struck with enough force to shake the palace before crashing back to the throne room floor in an open space twenty paces away.

Conryu stalked up to the throne and snatched up the black trident. It grew hot in his grip but he barely noticed.

Snarling, he snapped it over his knee and tossed the two pieces aside like so much scrap metal. With the trash cleared away, he dropped onto the throne and watched as Lucifer slowly regained his feet.

The fallen angel glared at him with glowing red eyes and for a moment Conryu thought he might actually attack.

Lucifer's expression quickly smoothed. He made his way closer to the throne, forcing the guards to move aside.

None of them tried to stop Lucifer. He was too powerful and would think little of destroying one of them. Or all of them for that matter.

He stopped in front of the throne and held out a hand. The broken trident flew over to him and fused back together like nothing had happened.

"Did you actually want something other than to pester me?" Conryu asked. "If not, I have things to do."

"I want the Reaper's power and I want you to give it to me."

Conryu stared at him, but he appeared serious. "No. Anything else?"

"Before you refuse, understand that my servants on earth can make life very difficult for those you care most about. Defy me and they suffer the consequences."

"You dare threaten my friends and family?" Conryu stood.

Lucifer flinched back a step.

Even the guards couldn't look at him.

The crimson light dimmed and black iron chains burst from the floor. They wrapped around Lucifer's arms, legs, and neck, binding him in place.

"You don't dare destroy me." Lucifer's deep, smooth voice held an edge of panic. "I'm too important to the master's plans."

Conryu clenched his fist and the chain around Lucifer's neck tightened. "By the power granted me by the lord of this hell I bind you."

Infernal runes appeared along the chains, burning red and steaming.

"You will not harm or work against me. You will not harm or work against those I care about. I bind you in word and deed." The chains tore free of the floor and wrapped around Lucifer, burning the runes into his flesh as he howled in pain.

When the chains had fused with his flesh and vanished, the normal light returned to the throne room. All the guards were on their knees, heads touching the floor. Lucifer staggered around like a drunk after a week-long bender.

"Now for your punishment." Conryu pointed and a black bubble formed around Lucifer. He made a fist and the bubble shrank to the size of a softball. "Cerberus."

The three-headed demon dog appeared not far from where Lucifer had hit the floor. His tongues all hung out as he panted. Conryu walked over and got licked for his trouble.

He patted Cerberus's muscular flank. "Good boy. I got you a ball to play with."

He tossed the bubble to Cerberus who caught it with his right-hand mouth, tossed into the air, and caught it again with his left-hand mouth. The middle mouth barked in delight.

Conryu left Cerberus to play with his new toy and returned to the guards. They were still kowtowing. Only Narumi remained on her feet, but even she appeared paler than usual.

"You all can stand up now." As they slowly regained their feet he turned to Narumi. "Sorry about that. I may have lost my temper a bit."

"Perhaps a bit," Narumi agreed. "But that's not why they prostrated themselves. For a moment, when you drew fully on his power, you looked like the master. Cloaked in darkness, the embodiment of death itself. I feared you might slay Lucifer on the spot. It is well that you didn't, and your binding was masterfully done though trapping him in the ball for Cerberus to play with might have been overdoing things."

Conryu shook his head. "No, that was important. For Lucifer, pride and power are everything. Once I showed him who had more power, I had to strip away his pride. Turning him into a chew toy just popped into my head at the moment. I'll leave him there until the Reaper returns. At least then I won't have to deal with him again for a while."

She smiled. "Fair enough. And at least you didn't turn him into a hamster. Now, shall we return to your studies?"

Conryu nodded and kept his expression even. Deep inside he silently wished another demon would show up and challenge him to a fight. At least that would spare him more lectures.

7

M iguel stood in front of the closed temple door and licked his lips. Since Baphomet made him his Chosen, he found he could see in the dark, albeit in shades of gray. That certainly made maneuvering around inside the dark temple easier now that the guiding light had vanished. He hadn't heard the voice of his new master since the ritual ended.

It seemed he had to proceed without guidance. Now he was supposed to go and slay the necromancer, a woman everyone in the islands considered just this side of a goddess, and not a friendly one.

His throat tightened and he forced himself to breathe. He wasn't Miguel the fisherman anymore. He was now the Chosen of Baphomet. He commanded powers others could only dream of.

In theory anyway. He still didn't fully understand how his new abilities were supposed to work. When the vines wrapped around him, no spells filled his mind. Other than the darkvision, the only difference was a sense of the growing things all around him. The plants were like glowing beacons in his vision. It was rather strange to be honest.

He straightened his new robe. No more standing around. He would learn through doing and hopefully not dying. "Open, uh, please?"

The door obliged, sliding out of sight and revealing the moonlit jungle beyond. It had seemed like his encounter with Baphomet had lasted hours, but clearly not. He stepped out onto the path and the door closed behind him.

Immediately, roars filled the air followed by crashing. Sounded like his pursuers from earlier were still in the area. Perhaps that was a good thing. He could practice using his powers on them before confronting their master. His racing heart argued that it was a bad thing and he should retreat back into the safety of the temple.

Another part of him, the part connected to Baphomet, understood that even if he wished it, the door wouldn't reopen until he completed his task.

None of this came to Miguel in words. It was all feelings and instinct. Crude certainly and far from precise, but he found he trusted what he felt. Why, he couldn't say. His mother, rest her soul, would grab him by the ear and twist if she heard such foolish thoughts.

The first of the monsters burst from the jungle. Miguel got his first real look at the thing. It resembled a gorilla, with a massive, hunched-over body, long arms, and a head filled with fangs.

It charged him, roaring, arms raised to crush him flat.

"Stop!" Vines shot out from every direction, binding the monster and lifting it off the ground. It thrashed but couldn't break free.

Three more appeared from a different direction. Ready this

time, Miguel pointed and the vines lanced out again, wrapping them up and dragging them over beside the first creature. Roar and fight as they might, the monsters couldn't break free of the vines. Which seemed impossible since the vines were only as big around as Miguel's thumb.

He couldn't just leave them hanging there. Killing the things would be no crime. In fact, he wasn't sure they were actually alive. Only uncertainty about how to do it kept him from carrying out the task.

Maybe he didn't need to think so hard about it. "Destroy them!"

Thousands of thorns grew from the vines which then yanked in every direction. The monsters were cut into hundreds of pieces that fell to the ground in a meaty rain. Suddenly being able to see in the dark wasn't such a great thing.

Looking hurriedly away from the mess he'd made, Miguel tried to figure out where he might find the necromancer. As soon as the thought appeared, he knew where she was, to the north and a little west. He sensed the building where it rested on the ground. She felt like a pitch-black presence moving around inside.

As best he could tell, the building was nearly three days' hike from the temple. Tromping along through the jungle for three days didn't appeal to him, but what choice did he have?

In answer to his silent question, thick roots burst out of the ground and wrapped around him. They dragged him down into the dirt. His darkvision revealed nothing but earth and stone.

The next thing he knew he was bursting up and out of the ground. Twenty strides ahead of him, a huge, sprawling mansion filled a clearing. Amazing, the roots had carried him all the way to the other side of the island in seconds.

Now that he stood facing the necromancer's home, his fear returned. Defeating her monsters was one thing, but the master was another.

Not that he had a choice. He knew as surely as he knew his name that failure would not be rewarded by his new master. That being the case, Miguel would just have to win.

———

Shesin Rhavia, better known to the people living on the neighboring islands as the necromancer, paced in her sprawling lab. Overloaded bookcases held centuries of accumulated knowledge. Two long tables were covered with beakers and vials for alchemy. All was cold and dark for the moment.

She'd received word from her agent in Hell that dark magic was about to change and if she wanted her spells to continue working, she needed to make alterations. At first, she'd considered it impossible, but when the appointed hour came and she tried the simplest of dark magic spells, it fizzled.

In fifty years as a living wizard and two hundred more as an immortal lich, she had never failed to cast Cloak of Darkness. That she failed today meant her agent had been correct.

Fortunately, the needed alteration was simple and she'd tested every spell she knew over the past ten hours and could now wield them all with no trouble. Just to be safe, she'd also tested magic from the other elements and found them still working properly.

While her imp had been correct about the change, the little beast had been less forthcoming about the cause. Whether it didn't know or the Reaper had forbade it to speak, she couldn't say. She'd sent it away with orders to find out what was happening and report back as soon as possible.

Now that she knew her magic was working, it was time to test her dark magic rituals. A powerful client was waiting eagerly to make the transition into an undead and she had a powerful artifact to trade for the privilege. Shesin wanted that item, but wouldn't get it if the client died and failed to revive. Galling as it was, she'd been forced to delay the meeting until she made certain she could deliver.

She moved to the center of the lab and raised her hands. Before uttering the first word of the ritual, she felt four of her guardians die in an instant. A frown creased what remained of her face. Her undead beasts were the most powerful creatures for hundreds of miles in any direction. She'd sensed an intruder earlier, but dismissed the arrival at once. She had unlucky guests wash up on her island from time to time. They made convenient snacks for the guardians.

Perhaps this was one she shouldn't have ignored. Anyone capable of destroying four of her pets was no mere lost fisherman.

Shesin lowered her hands. No further work would get done until she'd dealt with this pest. For the insult of interrupting her, the intruder would die slowly.

Leaving her lab, she made her way up a flight of stairs, down a carpeted hall, through the entryway, and out the front door. Standing at the edge of the clearing waited a lone figure, a man in his middle twenties dressed in a black robe with a strange red rune embroidered on it. As far as she knew there was only one man with power enough to defeat her guardians and this one was too old to be him.

Another male wizard seemed unlikely, yet there was no one

else on her island. Though oddly, this fellow didn't register as living to her magical senses either. A simple detection spell indicated he wasn't undead either.

Not living and not undead, that rather limited the possibilities. Demon maybe?

"Who are you and why have you come to my island?" she asked in Infernal.

The man cocked his head, clearly having no idea what she just said.

Not a demon then.

While she tried to figure out what she was dealing with he asked, "Are you the necromancer?"

The only one that would think to call her that was a local islander. No way did one of those people have power enough to defeat four of her guardians. "That's right."

"Good. I was afraid you were another guard creature."

The ground rumbled under her feet.

Shesin leapt back. Black vines tipped with thorns like inch-long blades exploded out of the ground where she'd been standing. They crackled with dark magic along with something else. Earth magic?

That couldn't be. Dark magic didn't mix with any other kind of spell.

The vines didn't stop moving so she could analyze them. They struck at her like serpents.

Shesin wasn't some amateur. "Wall of Fire!"

A barrier of orange flames blazed to life in front of her, incinerating the vines.

That was a relief. She feared the dark magic she sensed might negate her spell.

The ground rumbled again.

She didn't move quickly enough. An explosion sent her

flying backward. Stones charged with dark magic slammed into her undead body, bouncing off without harm. A living wizard wouldn't have made out so well.

After a single bounce she made it to her feet. "Fly!"

Wind magic carried her into the sky and hopefully out of range of whatever strange magic her foe controlled. Pity she couldn't use light magic, but maybe a wind spell would work. "Spirits of the wind be my sword. Wind Blade!"

A narrowly focused gust of wind powerful enough to cut a tree in half rushed out at him.

Instantly a wall of earth charged with dark magic heaved up in front of him, creating a shield. Her spell broke harmlessly against it.

So far, she hadn't noticed him chanting a single word. Whatever the nature of his power, it worked unlike any magic she'd ever encountered.

The wall of earth split, formed into balls, and shot up at her.

Taken by surprise, she ended up covered in dirt and battered by rocks. Though like before, her undead body proved too tough for the weak attack.

The intruder made a fist and the dirt covering her transformed into a band that started pulling her toward the ground.

She focused on her flying spell, but it lacked the strength to resist. Galling as it was, Shesin needed more than her natural strength. Pity she left all her magical items inside.

"Burst!" An explosion of wind magic blew the dirt off her body, freeing her from the spell. Before the stranger could react, she dove toward the shadow of a nearby palm tree. "Shadowgate!"

The darkness swallowed her up and she reappeared in her

basement lab. Now to collect the items she needed to teach this fool a lesson.

An earthquake shook the mansion. Pieces of the ceiling fell down around her.

She looked to the section of wall that hid her magical arsenal.

A floor joist fell with a horrible crash.

No time to get them now. "Reveal the way through infinite darkness. Open the path through the Reaper's Domain. Hell Portal!"

Nothing. Her spell failed.

Shesin snarled. She'd tested that spell not three hours ago and it worked fine. Why did it fail her now when she needed it most?

The obvious answer was the stranger outside had done something to block her escape.

A second floor joist snapped and fell, bringing a fair-sized portion of the ceiling along with it. One way or the other, it was time to go.

"Shadowgate!" She vanished into the same shadow she'd arrived in.

A moment later she appeared from the shadow of a different palm tree. For some reason short-range teleportation worked fine, but gates didn't.

Her train of thought was interrupted by a vine wrapping around her ankle. A second got her other leg and third the lower half of her face, cutting her off in midspell. She spotted the stranger watching from a few feet away, his face scrunched up in concentration.

More vines grabbed her and the earth opened up under her feet.

Slowly but inexorably, she was dragged down into the

darkness until all she could see was dirt.

Miguel watched as the top of the necromancer's head vanished under the ground. He did it. Somehow he defeated the most powerful person in the world. With his new powers he could do anything.

He grinned. From now on, life was going to be different. No more fishing out under the blazing sun, his hands dried and caked with salt and guts. From now on, he was going to be someone important. Someone to be feared and respected.

Congratulations on your victory.

"You're back! I...I thought you'd abandoned me after transferring the power."

No, but I had to see if you could act on your own. It was a test and you passed. Though she isn't completely dead yet.

"What do you mean?"

That creature was an undead wizard. She doesn't need to breathe so burying her won't kill her. But don't worry. The corrupted earth will drain the energy that sustains her unnatural existence. It will take time, but eventually she will simply cease to be.

Miguel wasn't sure he wanted to know the answer to his next question, but he had to ask. "What if I failed?"

Then you'd be dead, food for the earth, and I'd have to find a new Chosen. Serving me isn't an easy path. I won't lie to you about that. But it is a path to power and glory.

"Yes! Please, tell me what to do now. I want a new life. Something more."

Should you succeed in defeating all those who oppose me, you will rule this world forever. How does that sound for a new life?

It sounded very good indeed. "What do I do first?"

Return to the temple. I will guide you to the seeds of your victory. All you have to do is plant them.

Miguel didn't really understand, but he was willing to do whatever it took to please his new master.

8

"**E**nough." Conryu pushed away from the table in the library. After Lucifer's unwelcome threats had been dealt with, he and Narumi returned to resume his tutoring. Now he had so much new information sloshing around in his brain he could hardly think.

"We've barely even skimmed the surface of the other lords' powers and personalities, Chosen," Narumi said. "There is still a great deal left for you to learn."

"I have no doubt about that, but I need time to process what you've already told me. I fear if you keep shoving more in, some of what you already taught me will leak out. Just give me a few hours to rest and we'll get back at it, okay?"

She smiled, her perfect features lighting up. "Of course. When you're ready, summon me back. Rest well."

Conryu rubbed his eyes. He wasn't really tired, but he did want to lie down and decompress. He also wanted to not forget which of the lords was the hellfire one and which the fish one. He was pretty sure she said something about a torturer as well. Sounded nasty.

Did this palace even have a bedroom? Demons didn't need to sleep after all.

No sooner had he thought that than the library vanished and he found himself in a sprawling bedroom featuring an elaborate four poster bed with black sheets. The floor was covered in thick, gray carpet and a dresser with a fancy mirror sat along the wall opposite the bed. Somehow, he doubted the Reaper had a bedroom.

Wait. Did his will create this room?

He wanted a bedroom and boom, one appears. He shook his head and dropped onto the incredibly soft mattress. He groaned. It felt wonderful and was yet another thing he wished he could share with Maria.

Cool as it was, going forward, he'd have to be careful what he thought about.

He kicked his shoes off and swung his legs over with a sigh. He wasn't really tired, just overwhelmed. Who would have thought the universe was such a complicated place? Until yesterday, he believed that other than the elemental realms and wherever the elves had come from, the earth was alone in the galaxy. How wrong he was.

His eyes had barely closed when they popped open again. He'd asked Dean Blane to warn the governments, but did that mean all the dark magic users that weren't affiliated with a government would get the warning?

He didn't know and that bothered him. Someone could end up in trouble if their magic suddenly stopped working.

Plenty of dark magic users had agents in Hell. Ms. Umbra mentioned something about an imp. He had to make sure word got out about the workaround. And who better to spread the word than his own agent.

"Dark Lady."

An inky black pool of darkness appeared on the floor a few feet from the end of the bed. It elongated up and took on the figure of a bat-winged woman before vanishing and leaving the Dark Lady behind in all her stunning glory. She wore the thigh-high boots he'd gotten her for Christmas a few years ago and little else. A black leather bikini bottom and two motes of black flame completed her outfit. Pretty skimpy even by her standards, not that the meager garments didn't suit her flawless figure.

"Master." She licked her bloodred lips. "I knew you would eventually call me to your bedroom."

He sighed as she started to crawl across the bed toward him. "You're here for business not pleasure."

Conryu snapped his fingers and she vanished only to reappear where she started, this time dressed in tight jean shorts and a cut-off t-shirt that left her midriff bare.

She looked down at herself. "What is this?"

"Call it biker-chick chic. Anyway, the reason I called you was I'm curious if the other Infernal agents have been informed about the changes to dark magic."

She sniffed. "I don't associate with imps and other low-level riffraff. That said, rumor is, a number of agents from your earth have been hunting around for information."

Conryu nodded. "In that case, your job is to make sure they all know how to fix their masters' dark magic so it will work right. If you do a good job, when this is over, I'll summon you and we can have pizza at Giovanni's."

"Just the two of us? Like a date?"

He didn't think it was that big of a deal, but she seemed really excited, so he nodded. "Just the two of us."

She laughed and spun around. "I can wear my new outfit."

The Dark Lady turned serious. "You know, Master, that all

you need to do is give me an order and I'll be compelled to obey, especially now. If word gets out that you're really a big softy, you might have trouble."

"I already had trouble. Lucifer showed up and demanded that I turn the Reaper's power over to him. He even threatened my friends."

She winced. "I can't imagine that went well."

Conryu told her what he did and she laughed again. "You turned him into a chew toy? That's hilarious. He'll never live it down, especially after I tell everyone I know. You've absolutely made my century."

"I'm thrilled to hear it. Now run along, you have important work to do."

She bowed and vanished, leaving him alone again. He closed his eyes. Just a few hours of peace and quiet and then back to his lessons. Or maybe some horrid crisis would pop up.

He'd almost prefer it.

9

M iguel took a deep breath when the roots released him and he stepped out onto the loam of his home island. He'd gained and learned much in his brief time on the necromancer's island, but it always felt good to get home. He'd chosen a grove of palm trees a mile or so from his shack as his arrival point. It was midmorning and he knew no one would be around to see him appear out of the ground. He had also changed back into his ragged fisherman's clothes. He didn't know where the black robe went, only that it vanished at his mental command.

Hopefully his precautions would be enough to avoid a bunch of questions he didn't want to answer, not yet anyway.

A hundred yards separated him from the island's main dirt road. He stepped onto the rutted path and turned east. Not in any particular rush, he strolled along on the side of the road and considered his mission. In a satchel he'd found in the ruined mansion, he carried thousands of black seeds about the size of a sunflower seed. Baphomet assured him that anyone that ate one would be transformed into an obedient slave.

Miguel had no desire and more importantly no knowledge about how to command an army. Fortunately, in the absence of other orders, the newly transformed slaves would do their best to transform any uninfected people in the area. The process would be basically self-sustaining.

At the edge of a village made up mostly of one- and two-room shacks, a familiar voice called out, "Would you like to get rich and leave this dump? A few trips for us will bring you more money than ten years of fishing."

What good luck. The recruiters for the cartel were here. They must have an urgent load to go out as they usually never showed up until evening. Most of the fishermen would be out on the water already, but on any given day there were a few who, for one reason or another, usually a busted boat or swollen head, didn't go out. The drunks would be the recruiters' targets as a man with a damaged boat would be of no use to them.

In the town square, little more than a round dirt patch with a scattering of picnic tables, stood two men in rich clothes, their hair slicked back with grease, and wearing sunglasses that probably cost more than Miguel's boat. It was the same pair that always came. They never gave their names, instead letting the rolls of cash speak for them.

Today they had a crowd of one, old man Santiago, who spent more time in the village cantina than he did fishing. Of course, he was as old as Miguel's late grandfather, so no one bothered him too much about his shiftless attitude.

Miguel smiled and went right toward them. They would be the perfect ones to see Baphomet's seeds planted.

"Here's the fellow we need!" the older recruiter said, his red shirt billowing in the light breeze. "How would you like to make some real money, boy?"

"Actually," Miguel said. "I have a proposition for you. When I visited a remote island, I discovered a seed that had the most wondrous properties. You could sell them at a great profit."

The recruiters looked at each other then laughed. "We have all the product we need, boy. What we lack are couriers. If you're not interested, get lost."

"Please, sir," Miguel said. "Surely your employer would be displeased if you missed out on a new opportunity. Won't you come to my home and take a look? A free sample never hurt anyone. Mr. Santiago will still be here when you return."

Old man Santiago let out a belch of agreement before yawning and lying down on one of the tables.

"All right, boy, but this better be worth our time. If it isn't..." The younger recruiter reached behind his back and pulled out a silver pistol. He gestured with the barrel. "After you."

Miguel strode away from the town center toward his one-room hovel. He felt less anxious than he should have considering there was a gun pointed at his back. The powers he'd gained still remained largely a mystery, yet he knew that if he got into real trouble, all he'd have to do was think it and the two recruiters would be torn to pieces by vines. That knowledge did wonders for his confidence.

When they were out of sight of the village, Miguel stopped and shrugged out of his satchel. He held it open to give the men a good look at the little black seeds inside.

The older one reached in and pulled out a handful only to let them fall back inside. "What the hell are these? We can't sell dried beans."

They did look a little like black beans, Miguel hadn't really noticed that before. "They're not beans, they're dried mushrooms. You put one on your tongue and it rehydrates then dissolves. The high is unlike anything you can imagine. As soon as it wears off, your customer will be eager to buy more."

That sounded like a pretty good pitch considering he'd basically made it up on the spot. It was all bullshit, but they didn't need to know that. No one would ever want more than one, since after they ate the first seed, they'd be slowly transformed into something. Baphomet had been a little vague on the details beyond the fact that they'd obey Miguel.

"This kid's full of shit." The younger recruiter pointed his gun between Miguel's eyes. "I say we blow his head off and split. This miserable little rock is a waste of our time."

So much for doing this the easy way.

Vines shot out from the ground and wrapped both men around the wrists and ankles. The gun fell when thorns grew out. It all happened in the blink of an eye.

"I thought we could make a deal," Miguel said. "You get a new product and I get distribution. Clearly you're both too stupid to see an opportunity when it shows up."

The younger man opened his mouth and drew a breath.

A vine wrapped around his throat. "Keep quiet. I don't want you disturbing my neighbors. Now, here's what's going to happen. You two are going to take the product and get all your flunkies to spread it far and wide. Should you fail to make enough progress, I'll kill you both and find new dealers. Do you understand?"

They both nodded with enthusiasm, yet Miguel had serious doubts that they'd follow through once they were out of his sight.

You need to turn them. They'll be useless as mindless thralls, but I can teach you how to modify two of the seeds, so the curse works differently. Hold two of them in your right hand and we'll begin.

Miguel took out two seeds as instructed. A presence that

felt the same as the vine man in the temple took control of his mind and body. Miguel focused on the thoughts and feelings that appeared.

A dark aura formed around the seeds. The presence commanded the seeds to change from domination to simple compulsion. Anyone that ate one of the new seeds would remain human, mostly, but also be unable to defy any order Miguel gave them.

What a useful trick. Was there anything he couldn't do now that he had this power?

He could play more later. Right now, he needed to get his new servants off on their way.

"Open wide and say *ahh.*" When they hesitated, Miguel summoned more vines, these ending with four-inch thorns and hovering directly in front of the two men's eyes. "There are less pleasant ways we can do this."

With obvious reluctance, they both opened their mouths. Miguel put a seed on each of their tongues and watched it melt. They shuddered and their eyes turned fully black for a moment before returning to normal.

"You will go and spread the seeds to as many people as possible. Call them free samples, I don't care, just get them distributed. When they're gone, return and I'll have more." He released the men and sent the vines back out of sight.

The recruiters both fell to their knees but quickly scrambled back up. Miguel handed the satchel to the older man while the younger retrieved his gun. Neither spoke as they hurried away, leaving Miguel alone in the clearing.

"Where will I get more seeds?" Miguel asked.

You need to build a new temple, here. Once it's done, the blood of a wizard is needed to consecrate it. Then you can sacrifice the villagers and use their blood to feed the Black Eternals. The process is quite simple and don't worry, the temple need not be as elaborate as the original. In this holy place, the Black Eternals will bud and new plants will grow. More plants mean more seeds which mean more thralls.

The prospect of sacrificing the people he grew up with horrified Miguel and the voice must have noticed.

You owe them nothing. Who helped you when you were poor and nearly starving? No one. You serve me now and in their own way so will the villagers. Clear your mind of doubts or you will remain weak forever.

Miguel nodded. He would do what he had to in order to please his new master. It wasn't like he had a choice.

The Arcane Academy's library held thousands of books on every subject imaginable. Lucky for Maria, the ancient history collection only numbered in the double digits, fifty-four to be exact. However, all of them measured at least two inches thick. So far, she'd skimmed three in the hopes of finding any mention of names similar to the demon lords Conryu told them about. No hits yet, but her current book, a dry history of an expedition into the heart of the Amazon rainforest just over a hundred years ago looked promising.

She flipped the page and frowned at the drawing covering half the next page. It showed a temple, partially fallen but still mostly intact. The scientists dated it to nearly six thousand years ago. Apparently, they were shocked by how well-preserved it was for its age.

Maria skipped down to the caption. It read, Temple of Aberrant Fire. Aberrant Fire, that sounded vaguely familiar. She checked her notes. One of the demon lords was named Abaddon, Lord of Hellfire. That was pretty damn close. A language that old, if they didn't use magic, would have been easy to mess up the translation.

At the very least, it held enough potential to warrant a closer look. She marked her place, scooped up the book, and stood up. Her legs protested, sending pins and needles down her thighs. How long had she been sitting there? Too long it seemed.

The hall outside the library was deathly quiet. All the other students and most of the teachers had gone home for summer break. They also had instructions to keep their eyes peeled for anything out of the ordinary. While Maria would have appreciated some help in her research, Dean Blane had deemed it unwise to let word of the situation spread too far until they were sure how things were going to work out.

She turned right and walked down three doors. The viewing room was fully equipped for magical searches, including a six-foot-tall mirror enchanted to make scrying magic more effective. A lectern sat in front of the mirror and she set her book there with the image of the temple visible.

Using it as a reference, she pictured the temple as best she could in her mind along with the surrounding jungle. When she had the image fixed in place as well as she could she whispered in the language of wind magic, "Show me."

The mirror obliged to a certain extent. The jungle was there, but there was no sign of the temple. She focused harder, but the image didn't change. What could be interfering with the spell?

Maria walked around the lectern and placed a hand on the mirror's gilt frame. "Reveal all things hidden."

It was the most powerful detection spell she knew and it quickly did its job. A barrier was stopping the wind spirit bonded to the mirror from getting any closer. She shuddered and ended the spell. It had to be powerful dark magic to get a reaction out of her from so far away.

The barrier combined with the name of the temple made up her mind. "Kai?"

The ninja appeared and bowed. As always, she was dressed all in black and the lower half of her face was hidden by a mask. "How may I be of service?"

"I think I found a temple to one of the demon lords Conryu mentioned. Unfortunately, it's protected by a dark magic barrier. I was hoping you could take a quick look and let me know what's happening."

Kai shook her head. "The Chosen has tasked me with your protection. He would not be pleased were I to leave you unguarded."

Maria sighed then smiled a fraction. "You know he wouldn't mind if you called him by his name."

"So he has told me many times. Yet now that he sits on the master's throne, it would be especially disrespectful to show less than his due honor. As to your request, while I cannot go, he foresaw that you might have need of help. Melina."

A quartet of ninjas appeared behind Kai and bowed as one. They could have been quadruplets if you ignored the bust lines.

"We heard, Kai," the one slightly in front of the group said. "Where do we need to go?"

They all turned to look at Maria. She swallowed at the sudden attention. No wonder Conryu felt uncomfortable. Just five of the ninjas made her nervous; he was basically worshipped by almost a hundred of them.

"Um, Brazil, deep in the jungle. There's an ancient temple protected by a dark magic barrier."

"We should be able to detect a powerful barrier from the

borderland," the one Maria assumed was Melina said. "We'll pop out, have a quick look around, and report back before you know it."

"Remember what the Chosen told us," Kai said. "These are powerful new enemies. Take no unnecessary risk. If anything happens to any of you, he will be upset."

The new arrivals bowed and vanished, leaving Kai and Maria alone.

"Conryu really worries about you all."

Kai nodded. "He is a very kind master. Some of the other Chosen were cruel for the sake of it. All the Daughters of the Reaper love our current Chosen and would do anything for him. I'll resume my post until Melina and her companions return."

Kai bowed and Maria was alone. It pleased her that Conryu was a good leader and at the same time, the thought that all those beautiful women would do anything for him made her throat tighten. Not that he would ever take advantage of their devotion.

Of course he wouldn't.

———

Melina led her team through the borderland. Though everything was dark, she still had a strong idea of their location relative to the real world and the direction they were moving. After all these years no one had figured out exactly how that worked. The truth was that as long as it kept working, no one really cared exactly how it happened.

A shiver ran up her spine. Even at the very edge of Hell, she could feel the Chosen's presence in Black City. She'd spoken to him a few times and when she'd been hurt by the stone statues attacking their old home, he'd healed her along with some of the others. Melina had never felt such warmth and kindness from anyone and certainly hadn't expected to find that in the Reaper's Chosen.

She envied Kai getting to work side by side with him every day. Not that she would ever dream of complaining. Grandmaster Kanna wouldn't take that well at all. Their duty was to obey his commands, not grumble that they weren't getting enough attention.

Behind her Zan said, "Didn't the Chosen's mate seem a bit timid to you?"

"Kai says she's strong and loves him," Danner replied. "Maybe we just took her by surprise. Did you notice the circles under her eyes? I don't think she's been sleeping enough."

Melina looked back at them. "Hey! You need to focus. If anyone upsets the Chosen by getting hurt, I'll send you to the healer myself."

A moment later she sensed something powerful and alien. It was dark magic, but had a different feel than any she'd ever encountered. This had to be the barrier Maria sent them to scout.

"I think we're here," Zan said.

Melina nodded and drew her black iron sword from its sheath on her back. "Defensive formation. Assume there will be enemies."

The four ninjas stood in a square, weapons at the ready.

"Now!" Melina said.

She tried to shift back to the real world and failed. It felt like she ran into a wall. A dark magic barrier shouldn't be able to block them, but this one certainly had.

"What now?" Danner asked.

"Ease back." Melina willed herself to drift away from the

barrier and the others matched her, never breaking formation. When they'd put a mile between themselves and the barrier she stopped. "Let's try that again."

This time when they shifted, they appeared in a small clearing surrounded by jungle. A silent jungle. They'd all spent many hours training in an island jungle before they were forced to flee and Melina had never heard it as quiet as this. No birds called, no monkeys howled, it felt like they'd arrived in a dead zone. The plants thriving all around her argued otherwise.

Further away, the strange dark magic grated on her like an itch she couldn't scratch. Her heart sounded like a drum in her ears. Fear filled her and she didn't like it a bit.

"We need to get out of here," Zan said as her head swung back and forth. "Whatever's here isn't something we can deal with."

Melina understood now. The barrier not only blocked them from entering magically, but it must generate a fear effect. That must be why all the animals were gone. As soon as she realized the cause, her disquiet lessened.

"It's magic," Melina said. "Someone doesn't want us taking a closer look at that temple. Remember your training. You know how to fight this."

They took deep breaths and Melina sensed them drawing on their own dark magic to block the spell. She followed suit and after a few seconds was fully in control once more. At least there didn't appear to be any physical dangers, not this far out at least.

"We're okay now," Zan said at last. "Have you ever felt anything like that?"

Melina shook her head. "No and I'd just as soon never feel it again. The sooner we finish this mission, the happier I'll be."

Melina led the way back toward the temple. Each step felt like she was pushing against an invisible wall. Even knowing the cause, it took all her will to continue. There couldn't be more than a handful of wizards in the world capable of a ward this strong. Hopefully whoever made this one was long dead or at least many miles from here.

After a far-too-slow trudge through the jungle, they reached the edge of a ruined city. There wasn't much left standing of the smaller stone buildings, but the central temple appeared intact. It was a flat-topped model with stepped sides. The stones were black like a fire had scorched them. That had to be the target.

"Well, we found it," Danner said. "Do we keep going or report back?"

"The city seems empty," Zan said.

"Let's take a closer look. Other than confirming what Maria already knew, we haven't actually learned anything useful. There should be some markings or something on the outside of the temple. Maybe something that can tell us for sure what we're dealing with."

They shared a dubious look, but when Melina set out, her companions were at her side. That was a relief as she really didn't want to do this on her own.

The ruins were as silent as the rest of the jungle. A strange smell, like burnt... something, filled the air. The stench grew stronger the closer they got to the temple.

They reached the temple gate without getting attacked. While everything else in the ruined city looked ancient, the iron-banded wooden double doors appeared brand new. That implied that someone was either living here or had visited recently.

"Spread out," Melina said. "Look for anything useful. But don't get out of each other's sight."

She probably didn't need to add that last bit since there was no chance the others would separate in a creepy ruined city with a cursed temple. Still, better safe than sorry.

Melina stayed where she was and studied the stone frame around the gate. There were markings there, jagged shapes that meant nothing to her. Why hadn't she brought something to write with? She snapped her fingers and picked up a flat stone. With her black iron dagger, she carved copies of all the markings. Maybe they were decoration and maybe they were the secret of the universe. She'd leave it up to Maria to figure that part out.

"I found something!" That came from the fourth member of the team, Lin. She only joined the group a year ago, but she had a good head on her shoulders.

Melina carved the final marking, sheathed her dagger, and went to see what got Lin so excited.

The source of the excitement turned out to be a series of gruesome carvings depicting figures being burned alive in a giant cauldron. Even the Reaper had never asked something like that from his followers, at least not as far as Melina knew.

"What does it mean?" Lin asked.

"Nothing good." Melina looked at Danner and Zan. "Find anything?"

They shook their heads.

"Okay, I think we've gotten everything of value we're going to. Let's get back to Maria." When she concentrated, Melina couldn't shift into the borderland. While she'd hoped that the barrier only blocked entry, it had been a faint hope.

They set out for the jungle. A fifteen-minute hike should

get them out of range. While she was no coward, leaving this place behind would please Melina a great deal.

They'd barely managed a hundred yards when a crash sounded behind them.

Melina turned slowly, dreading what she might see.

Sure enough, the temple gate had opened, revealing the dark interior. Before Melina could even think of exploring the temple, a blue light blazed to life revealing a demonic skull seven feet off the ground. The skull was attached to a long neck that in turn emerged from a four-legged body covered in black scales.

She didn't know what sort of creature it was and she didn't want a better look.

It roared and opened its mouth.

"Scatter!"

Melina leapt right, just ahead of a blast of blue flames that nearly burned her legs off. As it passed, she felt powerful dark magic mingled with fire magic. That shouldn't be possible. Everything they knew said dark magic didn't mix with the other elements.

She sprang to her feet. Let the scholars worry about that. "Make for the jungle! Shift as soon as you're clear of the barrier. We'll gather in the borderland."

Her order given, Melina sprinted for the nearby jungle.

Another crash suggested that the demon was coming after them.

So much for the hope that it would stay to guard the temple.

This mission was going sideways quickly.

A gathering of dark magic was the only warning she got before another gout of flame roared out.

Melina dove.

The flames seared her back and she choked off a scream before leaping to her feet and continuing her mad dash through the jungle.

Trees crashed as the massive demon forced its way after her.

Melina concentrated, but she remained inside the barrier.

It couldn't be much father.

She put on another burst of speed, calling on her magic to strengthen her weakening body.

Dark magic gathered again, just as she felt an opening in the barrier. Wasting no time, she shifted into the borderland. Even in Hell, she felt the blue flames' passage though this time they did her no harm.

Drained and exhausted, she slumped. That had been far too close.

"Melina!" Lin hurried over to her. "Are you okay? Your back!"

Danner and Zan arrived a moment later. None of her companions appeared worse for the adventure, thank goodness.

Melina handed Zan the rock she carved the runes into. "Take this to Maria. I'm going to Black City. To the Chosen. I'll meet you back at the academy."

"Will you be safe on your own?" Danner asked.

A prudent question given that they were in Hell.

Melina managed a weak smile. "Who would dare harm one of us with him minding the throne?"

Her companions chuckled, bowed, and hurried on their way back to the academy. Melina turned her focus deeper into Hell and willed her abused body on its way.

Black City could be as near as a step or as far as eternity.

She hoped today it was close.

11

Conryu walked beside the Dark Lady down a hall that hadn't existed until he conjured it. It led nowhere and served no purpose beyond giving him somewhere to walk. He'd discovered as he spent more time in his current role, that the palace and most likely all of Hell would change depending on his whims. The idea that he might wish something important out of existence terrified him until he realized that anything he got rid of could be brought back just as quickly. The impermanence of this reality took some getting used to. He'd be happy to leave before he grew too accustomed.

"I finished spreading your message to all the agents I knew that are tied to wizards on your earth." She was still wearing the same biker girl outfit he'd conjured for her. It looked good on her but was a far cry from the usual outfits she wore.

"Good, hopefully that will make life easier for some of the dark magic users back home. I—"

He sensed someone in pain out in the borderlands. A human rather than a demon.

"Master?"

Conryu raised a hand to silence her and focused. Instantly he knew it was Melina and that she had been badly injured.

The hallway vanished and they were in the throne room. A moment later Melina appeared a few feet from him.

"Chosen?" She started to collapse but Conryu caught her and lowered her gently onto a mattress that appeared at his command. He pulled her mask down so she could breathe easier.

Melina's back had been burned to a crisp, destroying her uniform and reducing the skin to a blackened shell. He passed a hand over her, healing at the same time he tried to figure out what had caused the damage. He sensed both dark magic and fire magic mingled together.

"Narumi." The dark angel appeared at his summons. "What do you make of this?"

He pointed to a small section of Melina's still-damaged lower back. He'd blocked the pain, so his delay in healing it would cause Melina no discomfort.

Narumi knelt beside him and placed her hands on either side of the damaged skin. "Reveal."

A faint glow appeared then quickly faded away. Impatient though he was, Conryu held his tongue. When it came to detection magic, you just couldn't rush it.

Finally, Narumi said, "My guess is Abaddon's magic caused this. I can't guarantee it, but nothing else makes sense."

"The Lord of Corrupt Flames, huh? Does this mean the Reaper failed and the enemy has begun making moves on our world?"

Prime started to offer an opinion, but Melina groaned and tried to roll over. Conryu quickly healed the rest of her back and helped her get settled. Her head ended up on his lap, but he didn't mind. She finally opened her eyes and looked up at him.

Conryu offered his most reassuring smile. "Hello. Looks like you've had a rough time. Are you up to telling us about it?"

Her face reddened and she tried to sit up. With a gentle hand he pressed her back down. "Easy. I just finished healing you. No need to push yourself. Tell me what happened."

Melina calmed a fraction but remained tense. She told them about her team investigating a temple Maria discovered and the fire-breathing demon that chased them away. She ended with her decision to come to Black City to report to him directly.

When she paused for breath he gave her shoulder a reassuring squeeze. "You did the right thing, especially with those wounds. They were inflicted with dark magic and would have been difficult for anyone else to heal. I'm glad you're all okay, but from now on, if you investigate a suspected enemy location, take a larger force. You're all too important to lose to carelessness. I'll tell Kanna myself a little later."

"Yes...Yes, Chosen." Melina stammered and finally clamped her jaw tight. Conryu had never seen one of the ninjas so uptight. Then again, a near-death experience could affect people in different ways.

"If you're up to it, I'll send you back to your team. I'm counting on you all to keep up your good work. Please pass my thanks to the others."

Melina scrambled to her feet, seeming fully recovered now, and bowed so low that her forehead nearly touched the floor. "I'm honored to convey your message, Chosen."

Conryu smiled and waved his hand. He sensed Melina appear in the borderlands beside her startled friends.

His smile withered when he considered Melina's story.

Turning to Narumi he asked, "Now that you've heard her story, I repeat my earlier question: Has the Reaper failed and the enemy begun making moves in our world?"

Narumi shook her head. "It's impossible to say for sure. The demon could have been an ancient guardian that Melina and the others awakened. What concerns me more is the new door. The beast they fought couldn't have made it, which means someone else did and that they weren't attacked by the demon. That implies people loyal to Abaddon. In that case, we need to assume the worse."

"When will he return?" Conryu asked. "I'm useless to my friends here. Whatever's going on, I need to be back in the mortal realm to deal with it."

"That is equally impossible to say. The master will return when the conclave ends. Whether that happens in a day or months from now, no one can say."

Conryu bared his teeth and snarled. A few days was one thing, but if it took months for the Reaper to return, heaven only knew what he might return to.

———

Null's awareness floated in a dark pocket dimension connected to all the hells but controlled by none of them. It was neutral ground, a place where he could meet with his fellow prisoners without fear of attack. Not that Null was overly familiar with fear. Omnipotence tended to eliminate concerns over dying.

Though they had no physical form here, each of the psychic presences unconsciously formed insubstantial astral bodies for themselves. Null's cloaked form exactly resembled the real body he'd left behind in his hell. The others were the same, or so he assumed. They'd never meet in the flesh so to speak.

"Shall we move on to another matter?" Abaddon asked. The self-titled Lord of Corrupt Flames resembled a titanic skeleton surrounded by blue-black flames. The arrogant fool acted like he was the only one capable of conjuring hellfire. He might have the most skill with it, Null would grant that, but he was hardly their sole master.

"Let us discuss extending our arrangement on Earth 73," Null said.

"Soon enough," Baphomet said. The Lord of Corrupt Earth resembled a giant made of stone and vines. Null despised him and his armies of mindless thralls. They relied on sheer numbers rather than skill to defeat their enemies. The tactic disgusted Null, but he couldn't deny it frequently worked. "Surely there are other, more pressing matters to occupy us. A new contest perhaps. All our current ones are getting stale."

"We have over a million contests underway at the moment," Null snarled. "Earth 73 is mine and has been for five thousand of their years. I have no intention of giving it up."

"Perhaps not," Astaroth said. The Lord of the Undead and Disease resembled a giant vulture that walked on two legs like a man. "But we will see if you're strong enough to keep us from taking it."

At least they weren't pretending anymore. "You have no intention of extending our understanding."

"Of course not." Ardent Lilly, Lady of Lust, chuckled. She appeared as a young human woman in the prime of her life, all curves and sex and naked as the day she was born. Not that she could have any hope of seducing any of them, it was simply her nature to appear as she did. "You've had your toy long enough. Time to let others play."

"Then this meeting is over." Null tried to will his mind back to his body, but the others refused to yield.

"The meeting ends when we all agree and not before," Abaddon said. "We have to give our agents a fair chance to get started after all."

Null swore he'd see all their followers reduced to rotting corpses and in Astaroth's case piles of ash. Earth 73 was his. Nothing else was acceptable.

12

Kelsie had been listening in on her grandmother's conversations with the government, including three with the president himself. Nothing she heard filled her with confidence. Three new areas of concern had already sprung up. Miami was the one that had everyone the most worried. There was some sort of monster outbreak down there. No one seemed to have a handle on it.

The other two were outside of the Alliance and unconfirmed. One was in the Iron Lord's domain and as far as she could tell, everyone hoped they caused the immortal emperor a lot of trouble. The second was of considerably more concern. Someone calling herself Joan of Arc reborn was rallying former followers of the True Face of God cult. No one was certain of her intentions, but getting rid of one insane cult only to have a new one take over less than a year later wasn't a good thing.

Grandmother leaned back in her chair and rubbed her eyes. In the week-plus Kelsie had been with her, she seemed to have aged years. Her eyes were sunken in and her cheeks hollow. She ate next to nothing and slept little more.

"They're all fools," Malice said. "If the threat is of the magnitude we fear, there's no way these weaklings can protect the Alliance."

Kelsie licked her lips and asked, "What can be done about it? Elections aren't for another two years."

Malice's laugh was bitter. "No one electable will have the strength of will to do what's needed. If this country lasts another five years, it will be a miracle. Luckily, Kincade Industries is nearly as powerful as a small nation on its own. If we play things right, we could come out of the crisis even stronger."

She started coughing and Kelsie noticed blood on her hand. "You should rest, Grandmother."

"I have no time. Where is that god damn necromancer when I need her? She should know that if I die, she doesn't get paid."

The phone rang again. Malice took one look at the number and said, "Wait outside, girl."

Kelsie hurried out of the office and down to her room. Every once in a while Grandmother would send her away to have a private conversation. Kelsie didn't know who it was and frankly didn't want to. On the one hand, the less she knew about her grandmother's shady business, the happier she felt. On the other hand, what was the point of inviting her back home if there wasn't anything for her to do?

Anyway, this was a good chance to check in with Maria and see how Conryu was doing. She slipped into her room, and closed and locked the door before pulling out her phone.

Maria picked up on the second ring. "Hey, are you surviving your family?"

"So far. How's Conryu doing?"

"He's still in Hell filling in for the Reaper. And no matter how many times I say that I still have trouble believing it. We located a potentially active temple to Abaddon in the rain forest of Brazil. I don't know if that's something you need to share with your grandmother or not."

"I'll tell her and she can pass it along. To be honest, a temple in the middle of the jungle isn't going to be a priority for anyone." Kelsie heard her grandmother shout for something. "I've got to go. Tell Conryu I asked about him if you speak again."

"I will and be careful."

When it came to her family, she was always careful.

Kelsie hung up and pocketed her phone before rushing to see what her grandmother needed. Though if she was calling for Kelsie, it couldn't be anything important.

13

Jonny Salazar marched down the beach in his black boots and camo fatigues. Noon wasn't far off and the heat had him sweating like a pig. Eager as he'd been to get this post, he never thought much about the summer heat. Today the sun blazed down out of a clear blue sky and seemed determined to melt him. Even the always stunning beach bunnies failed to distract him from his misery. The lapping of the surf was so tempting it took all his willpower not to go for a swim, fatigues and all.

He'd been on duty for two weeks straight. Clearly the military didn't have a requirement that they take a day of rest. Of course, he was used to that by now. Like the rest of the guys, he'd bitch when he returned to the barracks. At least the zombie attacks had slacked off over the last ten days or so. That was rare enough and he wasn't about to complain.

Miserable as his post was at this time of year, it wasn't what really had him in a twist. Conryu hadn't made contact in months, not since the day he led his best friend into a trap. A trap that failed, just as he knew it would, but still.

He didn't blame Conryu for being pissed, but it wasn't like Jonny could ignore the orders of a general. The military was quite particular about that rule. Unless it was absolutely against the code of conduct, he had to obey or end up in a cell. Which might have been better than having his best friend consider him a traitor.

Oh well, it was too late to do anything about it now. He no longer had a way to contact Conryu. Which he couldn't deny was probably a good thing.

He paused and stretched. A moment later a scream rang out from behind him. He'd come to recognize those screams over the past year.

Jonny spun and drew his service pistol. Sure enough, a zombie was running after a trio of beachgoers. It was a quick one and looked fresher than most. Its skin still seemed intact and even its shirt and shorts were whole. In fact, they didn't even look wet.

Had it not come from the ocean? That was a first.

Whatever. Wet or dry, his job didn't change.

Jonny drew a bead on the zombie and popped it twice in the chest to draw its attention away from the civilians. Just as he hoped, the shots stopped it in its tracks.

He drilled it right below the left temple, blowing an eight-ball-sized hole in its head. The zombie howled and charged him.

Taken completely by surprise, Jonny dumped his entire clip into the creature, stitching up its chest and blowing its throat out.

It barely slowed.

What the hell kind of zombie gets a chunk of its head blown off and keeps coming?

They never covered this in training.

A quick reload and he was ready for round two.

Only fifteen paces separated him from the zombie.

Some kind of weird black stuff had filled the openings the bullets left.

Nasty.

Lowering his aim, Jonny went for its legs.

Ten rounds blew out both its knees and sent it tumbling to the ground.

It kept coming, pulling itself along with its arms.

Stubborn son of a bitch.

He backed up and emptied his second clip into its head, reducing it to pulp.

That slowed it further, but didn't stop it.

Slapping his final clip into place, Jonny finally remembered his radio. "Private Salazar to base. I need a burn team ASAP. I've got a stubborn one here that eats bullets like a cop at a doughnut shop."

"Roger, Private," the company controller said. "Team two is in your vicinity. Hold position until they arrive."

"Understood, holding position."

Jonny slipped the radio back into its holster on his belt and put a little more distance between himself and the still slowly crawling zombie. Assuming it was a zombie. He'd never heard anything about one acting like this. Sure, the fresher ones could take a hit better than the half-rotten ones that washed up on the beach sometimes, but two clips to the body and head? No way.

Lucky for him, the burn team showed up only five minutes later in their standard green Jeep. Four men in uniforms that matched Jonny's piled out. One of them shrugged into a heavy flame thrower pack while another helped him get it settled. A third man dug out a black bag that they'd use to carry away the ashes.

The unit commander, a corporal Jonny hadn't met, left his subordinates to their work and stomped over to Jonny. The corporal had a couple years on Jonny, but the nasty scar puckering the skin of his left cheek made him look older.

"Sir!" Jonny saluted.

"Private. What do you have here?"

They stared a moment at the still-struggling creature. In his head, Jonny had already reclassified it as something other than a zombie.

"Wish I knew, sir. I put two clips into it and as you can see, it's still moving. Thought maybe your guys would have better luck."

The corporal grunted. "Where's its head?"

"Blew it to kingdom come. Fat lot of good it did me. Do you know what it is?"

"Can't say as I do. There's always some new, nasty thing out there. This is the first time one showed up in our sector."

The burn team finished their preparation and Jonny gave them room. Blueish flames like a jet engine roared out, quickly reducing the creature to ash. They scooped it up along with the surrounding sand before hustling back to the Jeep.

"Orders, sir?" Jonny asked.

"Finish your patrol. You see any more of them, let us know."

That was it? Finish his patrol like nothing happened? "Yes, sir. Can you spare a clip? I'm down to my last one."

The corporal pulled two clips out of his belt pouch and handed them over. "Be sure to note this with the quartermaster when you make your daily report."

"Understood, sir." Jonny saluted before placing the clips in the empty holders on his belt. Relief washed over him when he was fully armed again. Not that the bullets were overly effective against whatever that thing he fought was.

He shook his head and set out on his route. What were the odds he'd run into another one today?

———

The rest of Jonny's patrol was blissfully free of unkillable monsters or regular zombies for that matter. He rode back to base with the rest of the patrolmen in silence, the Jeep overwhelmed by the stink of men who spent ten hours marching in the sun. No one else mentioned one of the new monsters and Jonny wasn't sure if he should either, so he kept his mouth shut. A rare bit of good sense, his CO would no doubt say.

The guards at the base entrance waved them through and soon enough the transport pulled up outside their barracks. A dozen guys piled out, eager to hit the shower and get headed over to the mess hall.

Jonny had barely taken a step toward the long, green building when the familiar voice of the base commander, Major Evans, rang out. "Salazar, my office, now."

He turned to find the major standing on the steps of the command building glaring at Jonny. He was pretty sure he hadn't done anything wrong. You couldn't tell much by Major Evans's tone. He sounded angry even when he was in a good mood.

At the very least, pausing for a shower wouldn't be a good idea. If the major wanted to find out what a day on the beach smelled like, far be it from Jonny to deny him.

He jogged over and saluted. "Sir?"

Major Evans led the way down a short hall to his office, a

utilitarian room with a clean desk, three chairs, and a small filing cabinet. Jonny stood with his hands clasped behind his back and waited for the ax to drop.

"I hear you did good work today with one of the unknown invaders, Private. Congratulations. The last patrolman to encounter one didn't survive."

Jonny kept his expression blank, but inside his mind raced. Someone had died fighting one of those things? He'd heard nothing about it and as far as he knew none of his company were missing. It had to have happened in another sector.

"Thank you, sir. What exactly are they?"

The major's eyebrows drew down. "No one seems to know. The wizards in the research department say they're working on it. In the meantime we can't exactly equip all our patrolmen with flamethrowers. And do you think they can spare us a wizard or two? No, just muddle through, same as always."

Major Evans was indeed in a foul mood, but it seemed Jonny wasn't the cause of it, which pleased him greatly.

"Anyway, that's not why you're here. As a reward for surviving, as well as your generally excellent performance over the last few months, I'm granting you a three-day pass starting at six am sharp tomorrow morning." Major Evans handed him a slip of paper which Jonny hurriedly accepted.

"Thank you, sir." Jonny saluted. This was his first pass in months and he meant it when he offered his gratitude.

"Hit the showers, Private. You stink worse than my wife's horse barn."

Jonny turned on his heel and marched out.

A three-day pass. He grinned. Time to raise a little hell.

14

Even standing in the shade of a palm tree, Miguel found the heat oppressive. For the past several weeks he'd been focusing on constructing the new temple of Baphomet. So far the villagers had raised the walls of the first floor and begun building the floor of the second, smaller level. He was mimicking the design of the original, though in wood rather than stone.

He'd been worried that his new master wouldn't approve, but the voice in his head assured him that as long as it was consecrated, a wooden temple would serve just as well.

His workers, on the other hand, had been less than eager to start their new job. Some had even laughed when Miguel told them what he wanted them to do. His temper had snapped, and the laughing man ended up impaled on a dozen black vines.

No one had laughed after that. The villagers all trudged out and started working with a distinct lack of enthusiasm. The first three days' effort produced almost no results. Annoyed, Miguel had ended up transforming the villagers into thralls. Now they worked nonstop without food, sleep, or complaints.

For a time, his conscience had pricked him, but that quickly faded. It wasn't like any of the villagers were family. Miguel had no family among the living.

A crash dragged his mind back to the moment. A log support had toppled, crushing a thrall under it. Miguel hurried over, but by the time he arrived the other thralls had tossed the log aside and the injured one regained her feet. One arm dangled limp and useless, but she had already rejoined the work crew.

Thralls really were so much more useful than living people. Maybe he should go to the next island east and convert them as well, that would speed the work even more.

As he contemplated this, he sensed two of his other servants approaching. Leaving the thralls to their work, Miguel walked along to the village dock. As he approached, he spotted a red speedboat slowing as it prepared to tie up. The two drug dealers he'd transformed, he'd come to think of them as Old Man and Young Man, were aboard. He sensed no anxiety in them so they must have good news.

When they'd tied up and got out onto the dock Miguel asked, "Well?"

"Master, we have sold half of the seeds," Old Man said. "The authorities have become aware of the creatures and destroyed some. Monster-to-monster transformations are proceeding quickly enough to make up for the losses."

Miguel nodded. When he concentrated, he could sense the numbers of Baphomet's army growing all the time.

They are your army as well. Take pride in all you've accomplished for your master.

He did take pride in what he'd become. Miguel had never

been much of a fisherman, but he seemed to be doing well as a hellpriest. He smiled. When the voice told him what his new position was called, he'd been delighted. His experiences with priests had never been positive, but he had admired the way everyone deferred to them.

And those were just weak fools with no power. You will be so much more.

"We have run into a more serious problem," Young Man said.

"What sort of problem?"

"Rival gangs are attacking and killing our street dealers. They seem to have figured out that whatever we're selling is transforming people into monsters. Monsters that don't buy their drugs. Without the support of our cartel, we don't have the strength to fight them off."

Anything that slowed the increase in his army couldn't be allowed. "You know where to find these enemies?"

"We know where some of their safe houses are," Old Man said.

"Good. I will come to the city with you. These obstacles must be eliminated."

If you could capture a few, they would make fine fertilizer for the Black Eternals.

That was a good idea. The plants were growing, but without a fresh source of blood, it was a slow process. An idea crossed his mind.

"Do you have a safe house as well? One with a basement?" Miguel asked.

"Several," Old Man said.

"Perfect. One of them will be transformed into a grow house. That will increase your supply of seeds and save trips back here. Once we have eliminated your rivals, distribution will increase."

The two dealers looked at each other, concern clear on their faces. They obviously wanted to say something but feared upsetting him.

"What is it?"

Compelled by his question Young Man said, "Our street dealers don't like selling the seeds. After a single sale, the customer never returns. We know why of course, but they think the seeds aren't getting people as high as they should. Increasing distribution could be a problem."

"Once the rival gangs have been dealt with, you will bring them to me and I will explain the situation. There will be no more trouble after that. I must collect the plants then we will travel to the mainland."

Both men lowered their gazes. "Yes, Master."

Miguel's smile broadened. How he loved to hear those words. In time, the whole world would say them.

15

Three days off. Jonny couldn't stop grinning as he walked down the quiet streets. He'd never gotten a three-day pass. In fact, he hadn't gotten more than a twenty-four-hour pass in six months. He intended to enjoy every second of it.

He took a deep breath of the cool morning air. He could hear cars in the distance, but this was a walking district which kept the noise to a minimum. The red-brick streets lent the area an old-school feel. It was much nicer than back home. He hadn't even seen any litter.

Some of the guys had been talking about a cafe around here that served the best ham and cheese omelets. His mouth watered thinking about something not cooked in the mess hall. Not that the food on base tasted as bad as people made out, but it was still cheap and mass produced.

Just ahead, a waitress at a little cafe was putting out tables and chairs as they got ready to open. He glanced at the sign over the door. It said, The Pig and Chicken. This was the place.

"Excuse me?" Jonny trotted up to the waitress who turned

to face him. She had bronze skin, big brown eyes, long, silky hair and a killer figure under her apron. The day just kept getting better. "Are you open yet?"

She flashed a bright smile. "Yes, sir. You can go right in and place your order. I should be finished out here in ten minutes. Then you can eat inside or out."

"Awesome, thanks." He grinned at her, but it was always hard to tell if a waitress was really interested or just looking for a better tip.

A bell chimed as he slipped through the door. Inside, a dozen tables were scattered around the dining room. The aroma of coffee mingled with something baking. His mouth watered as he walked back to the counter at the rear of the cafe.

He tapped the bell on the counter and a voice from the back said, "Just a sec."

The kitchen door opened and a woman he suspected was the mother of the waitress outside came out. She had flour on her nose and apron and a motherly smile. "You're from the base. You boys always look half starved when you come in here. What'll it be?"

"My friends recommended the ham and cheese omelet. I'll try that along with whatever sides go with it. And a cup of coffee please."

She turned and filled a mug from a carafe on the counter. "Here you go. The rest will be a few minutes. Sit wherever you like."

"Thanks." Jonny took the mug and found a table that let him watch the waitress moving around outside. She looked really good moving around.

He took a sip of his coffee and sighed. Was that even the same as the stuff they served on base? Sure didn't taste like it.

He was going to gain five pounds over his days off, he swore it.

A couple sips later, a man in a suit, his tie loose and askew half walked and half shambled toward the cafe. The waitress turned to speak to him, but he went right past as if not seeing her. He didn't look blind, which was the only way a man with a pulse could fail to notice her. Whatever had him worked up, it must have been serious.

The bell chimed as he stepped inside. The man stopped just inside the door, took one look around, and fell flat on his face.

"Ah, shit." Jonny leapt to his feet, peaceful morning forgotten. "Call an ambulance!"

He'd have done it himself, but didn't actually know the cafe's address. Kneeling beside the unconscious man, Jonny touched his neck. Still had a pulse, that was good.

"What happened?" He looked up to find the beautiful waitress standing over him.

"Beats me. He came in and immediately fainted." Jonny debating saying it was the sight of the stunning waitress that made him faint, but this didn't seem like the best time to flirt.

The older woman burst out of the kitchen, cellphone in hand. "They want to know if he's breathing and has a pulse."

Jonny held out his hand and took the phone. "The guy's got a weak but steady pulse and his breathing is shallow. His pupils? Just a moment."

He rolled the guy over. His eyes were open and black lines like thin veins ran through the whites of his eyes. He stared straight up clearly not seeing a thing.

"Fixed and dilated. I don't know what's wrong with him, but he's in a bad way." The wailing of a siren grew rapidly closer. "I can hear them now. Yes, ma'am. I'll stay on the line until the EMTs arrive. No, ma'am. I just have basic combat medic training. Yes, I'm from the base. Private Salazar."

The unconscious man started convulsing. Just as he was about to relay this fact to the dispatcher, the ambulance pulled up and the EMTs leapt out. Jonny hastened to get out of the way.

He disconnected and handed the phone to the cook. "Thanks for calling."

She nodded and put the phone in her pocket. "You handled that very calmly."

"I've been in a few stressful situations." He thought for a moment of all the things he went through with Conryu. "This one didn't rate that high on the list."

"Well, I'm glad you were here anyway. Omelet's on the house."

A cop car pulled up outside prompting Jonny to shake his head. "I appreciate that, but it looks like breakfast will have to wait. They're going to have questions."

Sure enough, a man and a woman in blue uniforms climbed out of the car and made their way into the cafe. The man motioned them over away from the EMTs who were working to get the unfortunate fellow on the floor loaded onto a gurney.

Jonny took the lead and when they got close the man said, "Are you the one that called it in?"

He nodded.

"Officer Sif will take your statement. Ladies, if you'll step over here." He led the cook and waitress a few feet off to one side.

He turned his attention on Sif, Diane Sif, according to the tag on her uniform. Jonny put her at about thirty, with short blond hair, icy blue eyes, and a fit if unremarkable figure. She was armed with the standard automatic pistol, cuffs, pepper spray, and extra magazines.

"Private Salazar was it?" she asked. "Can you tell me what happened here?"

Jonny did so, making a point to mention the black lines in the man's eyes. When he finished he said, "Not exactly how I expected my breakfast to go, but I'm glad I could offer a little help to that poor man. Dude looked like he had a bad morning."

"You've never seen him before?"

"No, ma'am. I work beach patrol and he doesn't fit the profile for what I see day in and day out. Too many clothes to start with."

Her stern expression cracked as she fought not to smile. Off to the right, the EMTs finally got their patient off the ground and were wheeling him toward the ambulance.

"What brought you to this particular cafe?" she asked.

"Some of the guys said the food was good. I haven't had a day off in months and a home-cooked meal sounded good to me. I certainly wasn't looking to start my morning like this."

"I imagine not. Okay, if I have any more questions, I'll find you at the base."

Before Jonny could say his goodbyes, a bloodcurdling scream tore the air. He spun to find the formerly unconscious man gripping one EMT by the throat and shaking him like a rag doll. The second EMT struggled to wrestle his friend free.

A backhand slap sent the would-be rescuer flying.

"Sif!" the male cop pointed at the chaos and she nodded.

"Stay inside and make sure the civilians don't come out."

"Will do," Jonny said.

Officer Sif ran out with her partner right behind her. Jonny never considered himself especially gallant, but letting your female partner go out first to fight a lunatic that appeared to be possessed or worse, seemed a bit cowardly.

The man finished with the EMT and tossed his limp body aside like so much garbage. From the angle of the neck, Jonny was pretty sure the unlucky EMT was dead.

A moment later he found out why Officer Sif went first. Instead of pulling her gun, she raised a hand and a gust of wind picked up the attacker and flung him across the street with enough force to smash in the door of a parked car.

Her partner ran across the street, gun drawn. He bent to check the assailant. As soon as he was within reach, the man grabbed him and slammed his head into the side of the car with enough force to crush his skull.

Even from a distance, Jonny could tell the cop was dead.

Officer Sif screamed and raised her hand again.

Before she could cast, the attacker leapt up and sprinted away into an alley.

She chased after him, alone.

That couldn't possibly be a good idea.

"You two stay here. I'll see if I can back her up."

He left the cook and waitress huddled together in the cafe and stepped outside. The EMT that took a backhand was slowly gathering his wits and, aside from a rapidly forming bruise on the side of his head and likely a concussion, seemed okay. He was certainly in better shape than everyone else on the scene.

Jonny left the EMT, ran across the street, and collected the dead cop's service pistol. Thank heaven for small favors, it was the same model he carried on patrol. He flicked the safety off and chambered a round.

Armed and as ready as he was apt to be, Jonny started down

the alley. He spotted Officer Sif around halfway down. It looked like she'd lost track of the assailant.

Keeping his pistol raised, Jonny scanned the area. There weren't many places for a man to hide. When he looked up, he spotted the target. The man was clinging to the wall of the right-hand building like a fly.

Jonny fired and the man fell.

The body was still moving, trying to get to its feet.

He kept firing. Three rounds to the head barely slowed him, confirming Jonny's worst fear. The poor bastard had turned into one of those things he'd fought yesterday.

Jonny dumped the rest of his clip into the monster's legs, keeping it from rising.

Officer Sif was staring at him, seeming uncertain what to do.

"If you know any fire magic," Jonny said. "I suggest you use it."

She shook off her stupor, pointed, and muttered some magic words. A stream of fire poured out of her finger and didn't stop until the monster was little more than an ashy stain on the blacktop.

"You okay?" Jonny asked.

Officer Sif lowered her hand and slumped. Jonny had seen enough of wizards to recognize magical exhaustion. Conryu could do way more than this without getting worn out, but it wasn't really fair to judge a normal person by his standard.

He hurried over to help but she waved him off. "I'm okay, thanks. How did you know what to do?"

"I fought one of those things yesterday. It wasn't quite as fresh as this one, but it wasn't long dead either. The burn team had to incinerate it to kill the thing. I put two clips in without much luck. Where are they coming from?"

She shook her head, unable or unwilling to answer his question. "We're going to have to fill out a ton of paperwork. You did steal an officer's weapon and discharge it in public."

"To save your life. And I'm not exactly a civilian." Jonny couldn't believe what he was hearing. Was he going to be in trouble for helping out?

"Hey, I don't make the rules. If it was up to me, you'd get a medal and a pat on the back. Now follow me. I need to call this in."

Jonny swallowed a sigh and fell in behind her. This was officially the worst day off ever.

16

The dealer's speedboat, a narrow red monster that roared like a beast and nearly flew across the water, brought Miguel to the Miami docks in less than a day. He marveled at the size of some of the ships they passed. Amazing what people could build if it made them money.

The sun had set when they tied up and no one approached their boat. That seemed odd. Surely there must be someone in charge of keeping track of comings and goings around here.

Their dock was little more than a long wooden platform jutting out into the water. It wouldn't have been out of place on one of the bigger islands. Certainly, Miguel had expected something fancier. But then again, what did he know? This was his first trip away from the islands and the world was a big place.

Once Young Man had tied them to a post sticking up alongside the dock, Miguel collected the box holding his precious cargo, a pair of the Black Eternals. The plants didn't handle light well, so he kept them tightly sealed.

"Where is everyone?" Miguel asked when they reached the end of the dock and stepped onto the pavement.

"The cartel pays the harbormaster to make sure no one comes near this landing," Old Man said. "It seems they haven't yet figured out our change in loyalties. Once they do, our deliveries will get more complicated."

"No, they won't. Not once I've had a private chat with the harbormaster. Now, there was mention of a safe house? I wish to get the Black Eternals set up somewhere safe."

"Yes, Master." Young Man pulled out his cell phone and sent a text.

Five minutes later, a boxy black SUV pulled up beside them. The driver, a man barely out of his teens with a beard and sunglasses leapt out and opened the back door for them. He couldn't have been Miguel's age, yet he already seemed to hold a position of some trust. Impressive.

Miguel and Old Man climbed into the back while Young Man climbed into the front with the driver.

"Take us to the Black Site," Old Man said.

"Yes, sir." The driver eased into motion.

Soon they were driving past massive warehouses lit by sodium lamps. Towering cranes jutted up here and there. Miguel could imagine what a hive of activity this place would be during the day. Once matters were under control here, he'd have to return for a look, just as a tourist.

Five minutes later they left the docks behind and entered the city proper. There were so many lights it almost felt like daytime. There were people everywhere. Strange music with a pulsing rhythm filled the air. He caught a whiff of some spicy food and suddenly remembered he hadn't eaten in days, maybe not since the day he became Baphomet's Chosen.

Such mundane mortal concerns are no longer a problem for you. Focus on your task and serve your new master well.

Miguel frowned. Would he never have to eat again? While that would be convenient, he rather enjoyed a meal with a glass of cold beer. Perhaps he could still enjoy them, but they wouldn't be necessary.

"Master, is all well?" Old Man asked.

Miguel forced himself to smile. "Of course, I was just thinking. How much further to the safe house?"

"Not far. Black Site is our most secure and secret base. It's only used for extremely important or dire circumstances."

"Sounds perfect for my needs."

They eventually left the light and noise of the city center behind and entered a residential area filled with row upon row of nearly identical houses. The SUV pulled into the driveway of a modest red ranch house and the garage door went up.

Miguel didn't know what he'd expected a cartel safe house to look like, but this certainly wasn't it. "Are you sure this is the right place?"

"Absolutely," Old Man said. "Where better to hide than in plain sight? The house is owned by a nurse with a perfectly clean record and no known connection to us. She lives here, comes and goes to her job, and basically leads the life of an ordinary person. It's a perfect cover."

"Why would she do this for us?" Miguel asked.

"A five-million-dollar retirement account in an offshore bank as well as our promise not to feed her to the alligators."

"I see." He got out beside a red coupe convertible. The nurse's he assumed. "What now?"

"Now we go to the basement and get everything set up," Old Man said.

Young Man and the driver led the way inside. As soon as

the garage door opened a muted crack sounded and Young Man collapsed, a red hole in his forehead. The driver ran inside out of sight.

More bullets cracked into the SUV.

Glass shattered in the windows behind them.

"Why am I being shot at in my new safe house?"

Old Man shook his head. He'd drawn his pistol, but so far hadn't seen fit to take a peek over the hood. Miguel didn't blame him. The bullets were coming in faster than the rain in a hurricane.

He drew a deep breath and reached out to Young Man's body. The altered seed still lived within him. A trickle of power caused it to spread beyond the body's brain. In seconds, the corpse was fully transformed into a true thrall.

"Kill them all," Miguel whispered.

The newborn thrall sat up and promptly got hit with a hail of bullets. While they did his clothes no good, the monster didn't slow as it plowed up the steps.

The hail of bullets stopped as whoever waited inside went from trying to kill them to trying to survive.

"Let's go." Miguel set the Black Eternals on the cement, stood, and strode around the SUV. He wanted at least one of the attackers alive.

"It's dangerous, Master," Old Man said.

"Not anymore. Your late partner is keeping them occupied. As best I can tell, there are four of them along with the driver. Do you have any idea who they might be?" Miguel stepped through the door and into a little hall connecting the garage to the house. The walls were riddled with bullet holes.

Old Man had his gun pointed down the hall, ready to blast anyone foolish enough to make themselves seen. "A hit squad from another group or maybe even our own cartel. We've certainly been acting in a way that would displease our former employers."

"That doesn't exactly narrow it down." Miguel felt one of the killers die and the spores immediately begin to spread through the body. He spent a little more power to accelerate the process and in moments a second thrall joined the battle.

They reached the living room and found little beyond spent shells and a blood trail leading deeper into the house.

A scream sounded as a second killer died.

That was enough for the others and they fled.

Miguel had no intention of letting them escape. He sprinted through the house and out the back door just in time to see three men piling into a black SUV exactly like the one that picked them up at the dock.

Tires squealed and smoked, but a dozen black vines had them by the frame and axle. Miguel pointed and more vines, thicker than any he'd created before, exploded out of the ground and smashed up through the hood carrying the still-screaming engine with them.

The doors swung open and the killers emerged guns fist. Smaller vines pierced them through the arms and legs. The guns fell to the ground.

"Step out now if you want to live," Miguel said.

The driver climbed out of the wrecked car, his hands over his head. "Please don't kill me. I was just following orders."

"Whose orders?" Miguel asked. "One of these fools?"

"No, the local boss. He controls everything in the state. I just let them know you were on the way, I swear."

"As if that's not enough?" Miguel pointed and a vine wrapped around the driver's neck. Thrones sprouted and the vine yanked back. His head landed with a wet plop. "Where can we find the local boss?"

"I know where he lives," Old Man said.

"Splendid. We'll need these two to help us get inside. Infect them."

Young Man's bullet-riddled corpse staggered toward the two bound hitmen and dripped blood onto their faces.

Miguel felt the spores inching through them and reached out with his magic to control the process. He needed more than mindless thralls for this task.

The hitmen screamed as thin tendrils burrowed through their brains and bodies. In less than half a minute he had them fully under his control. Their wounds closed, filled in by black tendrils.

"Command us, Master," the hitmen said in unison.

Sirens sounded in the distance.

"This place is no longer secure, Master," Old Man said.

As if it ever was.

"Is our vehicle still drivable?" Miguel asked.

"I think so, though we'll need to ditch it soon. Bullet-riddled cars tend to draw attention we don't want."

"Go get it. I need to explain to the boss how the new power structure works. And don't forget the plants."

Old Man hurried away.

Miguel stared at his new slaves and frowned. He was meeting more resistance than he expected.

The world will not fall easily and you have yet to encounter true resistance. Be patient. Don't let your anger dominate your reason.

If this wasn't real resistance, Miguel wasn't looking forward to see what awaited him.

17

Maria sat in her chair in the academy library and tried not to fidget. She had a notebook in front of her with everything she'd learned in the last three weeks. That consisted of three pages. Not exactly earth-shattering. Even worse, she'd pretty much exhausted all the applicable documents. She just didn't know what her next move should be.

To her left sat Dean Blane and to her right Ms. Umbra. Both of the older women looked perfectly calm. Maria liked to imagine they were as nervous as her, but she doubted it. Nothing like years of experience to keep you calm in a crisis.

She relaxed her clenched fists. At the very least she needed to look at ease for Conryu's sake. He was in charge of all of Hell as well as getting lessons about the other eight demon lords. Knowing how he felt about lectures, Maria figured he was tearing his hair out. She smiled and finally relaxed her tense shoulders. The image of Conryu yanking out his hair calmed her. Maria wanted to chuckle but held it in.

A little chill ran through her and a moment later the ring of black fire appeared along with Conryu's face. "Am I late? I keep losing track of time here."

"No, you're right on time," Dean Blane said. "How fare things in Hell?"

"Surprisingly boring. No one's given me a moment of trouble since I dealt with Lucifer. Now I spend twenty hours a day hearing details about the most powerful beings in existence. Which is much more tedious than it sounds. I hope you have some targets for me when I get back as I really need to blow something up."

They all looked at Maria who cleared her throat. "Unfortunately, since locating the temple in the Amazon, I haven't found anything solid. A couple of old legends sound promising, but they're not really old enough."

"Let's hear them anyway," Conryu said.

"I've got the minotaur which sounds like it could be a version of the Horned One. And then there's the Kraken, which makes me think of Dagon. For the minotaur I'd suggest looking at Crete. As for the Kraken, I have no idea. It's a common myth in multiple countries."

Conryu nodded, seeming unbothered by her relative lack of information. "That's something anyway. Narumi has next to nothing about the other lords in the library here. She says one of the things they all get good at quickly is protecting themselves from opposing forces. I assume that means powerful wards and killing anyone that stumbles across their temples. I'm very impressed that you uncovered Abaddon's temple. That was well done."

Maria smiled. He always knew how to make her feel better. "Thanks. I almost hate to make my next suggestion."

"This is no time to be shy," Dean Blane said. "Let's hear it."

"I want to consult with Professor McDoogle. When it

comes to esoteric knowledge, he's the best source I can think of." Seeing Conryu's expression she hastened to add, "I won't tell him anything important. If it doesn't work out, I have no more ideas."

Conryu looked like he'd swallowed something bitter. "Fine. It's not like I have to talk to him. And no mention of me running Hell. I can just see the title of his next book. Merlin's Heir Goes to Hell or something equally stupid."

"Not a word, I promise," she said.

"Okay. Hopefully the next time we speak it will be in person. I can't believe the Reaper's meeting could last much longer."

"Don't be too sure," Ms. Umbra said. "Remember, beings like him live on a time scale we can't begin to comprehend. A short visit to them might be months or years to us."

Conryu grimaced. "On that cheery note, I'll bid you ladies good evening."

When he'd gone Maria sighed. While she didn't dislike Angus as much as Conryu, she did find the old man tedious. Hopefully he'd have some information that would make the visit worthwhile.

———

Maria ended up needing a couple hours to track down Angus's new place. He wasn't listed anywhere as the renter of an apartment, but with the help of Mrs. Koda's government friends, she traced him to a run-down apartment building in a rough part of south Sentinel City.

Traveling via a Heaven portal, she emerged on the sidewalk facing a seven-story tenement covered with graffiti. She'd seen worse places, but that was in a documentary covering a war zone.

Why in heaven's name would Angus live in a place like this? Had he really fallen on such hard times after the business with Atlantis? At the very least he should still have royalties to keep him comfortable.

A gun shot sounded in the distance prompting Maria to cross the street and get on with her business. Before she could enter the building a faint chill heralded Kai's appearance.

The ninja bowed. "Do you wish me to walk with you? There may be some danger."

"Barring a serious magical attack, I'll be fine. I know I'm not as strong as Conryu, but I'm not that weak."

"I meant no disrespect," Kai said.

Maria sighed. "I know and I appreciate the concern. But I really will be fine."

Kai bowed again and vanished. Though she was no longer physically present, Maria couldn't help feeling better knowing she was only a thought away should there be serious trouble.

Maria pulled the door open and stepped into a foyer filled with empty beer bottles and used syringes. More grateful than ever for the invisible light magic barrier surrounding her, Maria headed for the stairs. Angus lived on the top floor, but she wouldn't trust the elevator in a place like this. Besides, a little exercise would do her good and give her time to finalize her pitch.

Angus's ego was his weak spot. A few compliments on his great intelligence should do the trick.

She stepped over an unconscious man in the middle of the fourth floor landing and made an effort not to step in whatever stained the boards around him.

Maria made it to the seventh floor without encountering

anyone conscious. She also hadn't heard any screams, blood-curdling or otherwise. What would this place be like at night? She shuddered to think.

A trio of cockroaches skittered out of sight when she stepped onto the seventh-floor landing. Angus lived in apartment 7-3. She went right and soon found it.

She knocked twice before a voice shouted, "Go away!"

"Professor McDoogle? It's Maria Kane, Conryu's girlfriend. I need your help. Can you spare a moment? Please?"

There was a long pause and for a second she feared he might just ignore her. She was weighing the best spell to force the door when it opened four inches and a bloodshot eye peered out.

"I remember you. Your ingrate boyfriend never did appreciate all I did to make him famous. What do you want?"

"A consultation. Can I come in? I don't want to bother anyone."

"You won't bother anyone. They're all passed out most days until noon. High on whatever flavor of drug they medicated with the night before." Angus finally opened the door. "Well, come in if you're coming."

Maria slipped inside and the door slammed shut behind her, the locks clunking into place. "Thank you, Professor."

She looked around at his new home and struggled to keep her distaste from showing. There wasn't much in the way of furniture, just a sofa and dining room table. The kitchen looked like no one had cleaned in weeks and a sour smell filled the air.

In the end, the only thing that interested her was the pile of several hundred books stacked against the wall. There had to be something of use there.

"Bah. Just Angus is fine. No school will have me after

Atlantis and no publisher will touch my book on the subject. I'm sure the government has told them all to keep it quiet. Those pricks are always covering something up. What did you say you wanted?"

"I'm researching ancient cults, anything over five thousand years old. Given your knowledge of esoteric subjects, I thought calling on you would be a smart move."

"Ancient cults, huh. Something for the academy?"

Maria nodded. That wasn't the whole truth, but close enough. "I started working on it before graduation and they let me stay behind to finish up. Unfortunately, the library has a surprisingly sparse collection on the subject."

"I'm not surprised." Angus went over to his tower of books and started reading the spines. "Modern magic is largely focused on new advances rather than on history. A bit of a blind spot in my opinion, but then again no one ever asked. It's nice to see a young scholar interested in history. Most of my own research is focused on the past. Here we are."

He pulled a book out of the second tower, being careful to keep the rest from ending up on the floor. It was a slim volume, less than an inch thick, with a battered cover that had worn so much the board showed through the cloth. There were no markings on the cover or spine to indicate the contents.

"What is it?" Maria asked as she accepted the tome.

"A journal written by a millionaire obsessed with history. He funded numerous expeditions around the world about two centuries ago. This is a record of everything they found. The entries aren't as detailed as I'd have liked, but it should give you a starting point."

"This is fantastic," Maria said. "Thank you. Can I keep it for a day and make copies? I'll return the original tomorrow."

"On one condition."

Maria didn't like the way he said that. "What is it?"

"My Atlantis book doesn't have an ending. No one will ever publish it, but for my own peace of mind, I'd like to know what happened to the city."

No one had told her to keep what happened a secret. It wasn't like anyone could reach Atlantis now. "Alright. It's gone. Conryu shifted it into a pocket dimension where no one can get to it and the many dangerous secrets hidden there."

Angus smiled and shook his head. "Of course he did. I imagine the various world governments were thrilled to lose all those potential advances. Is there anything that boy can't do?"

"I certainly hope not since he's often the only thing between us and the latest horror trying to destroy or take over the world."

"Good point and good luck with your research."

"Thanks. I'll be back tomorrow with your book."

He waved her off which surprised Maria. "Take your time. My days of chasing down mysteries are over. After Atlantis, I officially retired."

"Enjoy your retirement then." Maria opened a Heaven portal and returned to the academy. She had a lot of reading to do.

18

A yellow taxi dropped Jonny off in front of the base at ten minutes to noon. He'd spent most of the past four hours at the local police precinct going over and over everything that had happened at the cafe that morning. At least they hadn't given him any shit about borrowing the dead cop's pistol. In fact, the lieutenant had been grateful that he'd stepped in to back up their officer. As far as they were concerned, the only thing worse than a dead cop was two dead cops.

When he'd tried to sneak a question or two in, all he'd gotten was evasions and outright refusals to comment. Ongoing investigation he said, couldn't comment. So Jonny had returned the favor when questioned about any encounters he might have had on the beach. The good lieutenant hadn't liked that nearly as well.

That was too bad. If he wanted more intel, he could get it from Major Evans. He'd finally been released and given a free taxi back to base. His stomach complained about the stale doughnut and bitter coffee that had replaced his omelet for breakfast. Even lunch at the mess hall would be welcome.

Jonny trudged up to the gate and offered the sergeant on duty a halfhearted salute.

"Salazar," the middle-aged sergeant said. "Thought you were on a three-day pass."

"I am, but something came up and I need to report to Major Evans. Please tell me he's on base."

"All I can say is he hasn't left by this entrance." The sergeant pressed a button in the gatehouse and the wooden barricade rose out of Jonny's way.

"Thanks, Sarge." Jonny jogged through and turned toward the command center. If the major wasn't there, they'd know where to find him.

Ten strides from the command center, the door opened and Major Evans himself emerged. He spotted Jonny approaching and frowned. "Private, you're the last person I expected to see today."

"Same here, sir. But I had the misfortune to encounter a relative of the monster I met yesterday."

The major's frown deepened. "My office, now."

Once again Jonny found himself standing at parade rest, hands clasped behind his back, in front of the tidy desk while the major stared up at him.

Instead of asking immediately about the monster he said, "What is it with you, Salazar? Everywhere you go, trouble follows. Did that wizard friend of yours hex you or something?"

"Not so far as I know, sir. Conryu's not the sort to do something like that and I haven't even seen him since the incident last year."

Major Evans ran a hand across his face. He looked about ten years older than he had earlier. "Well, tell me everything."

Jonny did so. When he finished, he added, "I figured you wouldn't want me talking out of turn about our encounters with those things."

"You were right. Still, I can't believe no one sent us a notice that they'd spread through the city. Clearly they're not getting washed up on the beach like regular zombies." The major's jaw bunched and relaxed as he chewed over this new information.

"What should—"

The phone rang, cutting him off in mid question.

The major picked it up on the second ring. "Evans."

Jonny backed up a step, but Major Evans raised a hand then pointed at an empty chair. A sick feeling twisted his stomach, but he didn't dare leave. The chair's squeak when he sat seemed especially loud in the quiet office.

"Yes," the major said. "Word of the encounter just reached me. You're quite right, he's an excellent soldier. A joint investigation sounds fine to me. He'll be ready."

Major Evans hung up. "I'm revoking your pass. In one hour someone from the Miami Metro will be here to pick you up to begin a joint investigation. Anything you learn, you tell me. They've kept enough secrets. I don't care if the city isn't our jurisdiction. We've got far more resources to figure out what's really happening."

"Sir, the whole joint task force is me and one of their people?"

"Yes. We can't spare anyone else and from the sounds of it, they can't either. Whatever's really going on, the cops are barely keeping it under control."

"Permission to get something to eat and take a shower before my new partner arrives?"

"Granted. Meet them at the main gate. Civilians aren't allowed on base."

"Yes, sir." Jonny saluted and hurried out.

So much for his time off.

J onny stood by the gate, fed, showered, and most importantly armed. He had his standard pistol, two clips in their holders, and six more stuffed into the zippered pockets of his fatigues. He felt human again and even though his vacation had only lasted half a day and included a gun fight with a nearly unkillable monster, he was kind of relieved to have a mission.

He didn't know exactly how much time had passed, but a blue and white police car finally stopped in front of the main gate. A familiar face framed by short blond hair stared out of the driver-side window at him.

Jonny marched over and she rolled down the window. "Officer Sif. Looks like we're partners for the time being."

"Looks like." She sounded neither angry nor bitter about the situation, so that was a good start. "When they told me I was teaming up with someone from the base, I didn't think it would be you. At least I know you can shoot. Jump in."

He went around and settled into the passenger-side seat. "We can all shoot. That's the minimum qualification to be a soldier."

"You got me there." She put the car in gear and did a U-turn back toward the city. "I suppose our adventure this morning convinced the powers that be that keeping each other in the dark wasn't in anyone's best interest."

"No, in fact I have orders to tell you no more than I have to and to report anything you tell me back to my commanding officer. I fear the idea of actually working together is lost on Major Evans."

She laughed. "My captain told me the exact same thing. Why are you ignoring your orders?"

In for a penny in for a pound. "Because whatever's going on is big. I don't know yet what it is exactly, but it's not some little thing. My job is to protect people, the same as yours. I couldn't live with myself if someone else died because some bureaucrat didn't want to play nice with a rival for funding. I'll be straight with you if you return the favor."

"Deal. I hate the politics too. You want to go first or should I?"

"I will. I ran into one of those things yesterday on the beach. Thought it was just another zombie until I couldn't kill it. Nothing would stop it except the flame thrower. Major Evans said the military's wizards are trying to figure out what they are but so far no luck."

"Would he tell you if they had figured out what they are?"

"Good point, but I think at the very least they'd tell us how to better kill them. Your turn."

She rounded a corner a bit too fast and Jonny hastened to fasten his seatbelt. "They started showing up about two weeks ago. Just one or two at first. Three patrolmen ended up dead before we learned just how dangerous they are. Now as soon as one is spotted, a wizard is called in, usually a light magic specialist. Unfortunately, we only have two and they're on the verge of collapse. My superiors were delighted when I told them fire works nearly as well. On the downside, you have to be much more careful where you use fire magic."

"You don't know where they're coming from either?" Jonny asked.

Officer Sif shook her head. "I wish I could say otherwise, but we have no idea. The first ones we encountered were in the slums downtown, but since then they've cropped up everywhere. The one this morning is the first anyone has seen transform. Usually when we get called in, they're already in full monster mode."

Major Evans wasn't going to be getting a very satisfying report this evening. They pulled off the road in front of a modest duplex. Officer Sif checked the map on her console then looked at the house then back.

"Something wrong?" Jonny asked.

"No, this is the place. I just assumed from his suit that he might have lived somewhere nicer."

"Maybe he spent all his money on clothes. Good part about being in the army, they provide all the clothes you'll ever need. Let's go see who's home. I really hope there aren't kids."

"Me too. Death notifications are something I'll never get used to. Usually I'm the junior officer and all I have to do is stand quietly. This is my first time as lead."

"If it makes you feel any better, it's my first time going to a notification, so we'll figure it out together."

They crossed the street and climbed the stairs in front of the left-side door. She knocked and a few seconds later a haggard woman with dark skin and frazzled hair opened the door.

The woman took one look at Officer Sif and said, "He overdosed, didn't he? I knew Amelio would end up like this. I warned him, you know. Over and over."

"No, ma'am, he didn't overdose." Officer Sif said. "He

collapsed at a cafe called The Pig and Chicken. By the time the ambulance arrived it was too late."

Jonny thought that was a gentle way of describing what happened, but he kept his hands clasped and his mouth shut. In the army you got lots of practice doing that.

"Maybe it wasn't an overdose, but the drugs must have caused whatever happened to him."

"Would it be okay if we came in, Mrs. Lopez?" Officer Sif asked. "If you tell us more, maybe we can find whoever sold your husband the drugs that killed him."

She slumped in the doorway and shifted to one side, just enough to let them pass. Clearly her husband had put her through a lot. Jonny had never seen anyone as exhausted as she looked. He had no idea what he could say to help so he stayed silent.

They went to a modest living room and sat on the couch facing Mrs. Lopez, who perched on a chair and looked like nothing so much as a bird ready to leap into the air at the slightest hint of danger. All around no decorations covered either the wall or the shelves of a nearly empty bookcase. The place seemed less like a home than a rental. There was no personality.

"Why don't you start at the beginning?" Officer Sif asked.

She laughed, humorless and bitter. "The beginning? Well, when we got married he was a sweet, honest, hardworking guy. Nothing glamorous, Amelio sold insurance, but it put food on the table. At least it did until the company switched to a commission model. That didn't suit his style and the pressure built. I don't know who sold him the first joint, but he quickly graduated to cocaine. It gave him energy and he made more sales, but he snorted most of the extra money. Things have been going downhill for a while now."

"You have no idea who his supplier was?" Officer Sif asked.

"No, though my guess is someone at his office. What could be a better place to sell cocaine?"

"Where did he work exactly?"

"Goodway Insurance. They're in a building downtown. I can look up the address for you."

Mrs. Lopez started to get up but Officer Sif waved her back down. "We can find it, thank you. And I'm so sorry for your loss."

Mrs. Lopez slumped back in her chair. "I lost him a long time ago. This just makes it official."

"Can we call someone for you?"

Mrs. Lopez shook her head. "I'll be fine. Please lock the door on your way out."

Jonny stood and followed Officer Sif out, locking the door behind him. "That was depressing."

"No kidding. Let's go see what's happening at the insurance office."

"Sounds good, Officer." Jonny got in the squad car and closed the door.

"You can call me Diane." She started the car and set out across town.

Luckily the streets weren't terribly busy and they made good time. Two blocks out from the office, they ran into a line of cars stopped in the street.

"What's this about?" Jonny asked

"Beats me." Diane grabbed her radio, called in to the station and gave the address. "What's going on down here?"

"There's been an incident at Goodway Insurance, multiple casualties. Survivors indicate a supernatural element. SWAT augmented by wizards is preparing to breach."

"This can't be a coincidence," Jonny said.

"No." Diane flipped her siren on and they inched through the slowly forming gap. "Whatever's happening, we need to be there."

Jonny nodded, but he had a really bad feeling.

19

Ten blocks from the so-called safe house, Old Man pulled over beside a park. It wasn't terribly impressive, just a square of grass with a trio of picnic tables and a sand box. Their shot-up SUV was still running, though barely. In the back seat, his new slaves sat in total silence. A normal person probably would have found it unnerving. Miguel just ignored them and focused on the next step in his task.

"Why did we stop?" Miguel asked.

"Don Carlos lives in a penthouse near the city center. We can't drive into that part of the city in a car that looks like this. We need to find a replacement."

Miguel looked up and down the street. There wasn't a car in sight. Across the street were a few dark, closed-up stores, but that was it. "And you chose this place to abandon the car why?"

"No security cameras, no witnesses. I know it isn't ideal, Master, but this is the safest place."

Miguel believed him, but out of curiosity asked, "How do you know that?"

"We dump cars in this area all the time. One of our guys smashes any cameras they install the same day. Nobody's bothered with a new one in months."

"Be that as it may," Miguel said. "It gets us no closer to new transportation."

A loud metal clatter filled the air behind them. Someone had raised a door and light shone out.

"Hey!" A shadow passed in front of the light as a shouting man emerged waving a baseball bat. "I've had enough of you punks ditching your cars in front of my place. I've been waiting for this moment. Now you're going to get it."

Miguel turned to the left-hand thrall. "Kill him and see if there's a car behind that door."

The killer climbed out of the SUV, pulled his pistol, and fired a single round through the angry fellow's head, dropping him on the spot. Holstering his pistol, the thrall disappeared into the building.

Miguel shook his head at the waste. He should have said to kill him with his bare hands or a bite so a new thrall would be born. That was the problem with the stupid things. If you weren't precise with your orders, the results could be iffy at best.

Happily, a moment later a motor roared to life and an old-fashioned car with fins on its rear panels backed out of the door. "Not exactly subtle, but at least there're no bullet holes in it. Let's go."

They swapped cars and were on their way again. Old Man had taken the driver's seat since he was the one that knew where they were going. Miguel paid no attention to the city around them. He hadn't used this much magic since his battle with the necromancer. That battle had left him tired, but this time he felt fine.

You're getting used to your new abilities and your body is adapting to the dark magic coursing through you. Over time your control over your power will continue to grow. Never forget this is a long game and you can't win if you're dead. Keep your risks to a minimum.

Miguel frowned. He'd yet to encounter anything in the city he considered a real threat. He seriously doubted the thugs' guns would have harmed him much. He didn't know for sure, but it was a feeling he got. He felt stronger than he'd ever imagined possible.

Around fifteen minutes after swapping cars, Old Man pulled out of traffic and down a ramp into a parking garage built beneath a towering apartment building. It had to be forty stories if it was one. After a couple laps, they found a parking space and pulled in.

Miguel climbed out of the car and asked, "Where to now?"

"The boss has a private elevator to the top floor," one of the failed assassins said. "There's a camera and if they don't recognize you, the door won't open."

"Prudent. Lead the way." Miguel fell in behind the assassins and Old Man brought up the rear carrying the box holding the Black Eternals.

When they rounded a corner the assassin said, "Wait here. If the guards see you, they won't activate the elevator."

Miguel stepped back and waited. Under other circumstances he might have feared betrayal, but those two were incapable of betraying him; his magic prevented it. There were voices but he couldn't make out what they were saying. As long as they got the doors open, he didn't care what they said.

At last a chime sounded and an assassin said, "Master, the elevator is here."

Miguel and Old Man hurried around the corner and the four of them stepped into the elevator. It was paneled in gold and the floor was covered in hardwood. The elevator was nicer than the shack Miguel used to live in back home.

There were no buttons and as soon as the doors closed they started up. The ride was silent and despite his considerable abilities, Miguel found himself getting anxious. He stomped mercilessly down on the feeling. He was the Chosen of Baphomet and no drug-pushing thug was a match for him.

Still, as the voice said, better safe than sorry. Miguel shifted and pressed his back flat against the wall so any incoming fire wouldn't hit him.

It was well that he did.

The instant they stopped and the door chimed open, a deafening hail of gunfire slammed into the back wall, much of it passing through his new thralls. Happily they were undeterred by such weak attacks.

His assassins drew their weapons and returned fire.

Miguel sensed something he'd never felt before.

Someone's casting a spell. Protect yourself.

Miguel wrapped himself and Old Man in a cocoon of vines an instant before a river of fire filled the elevator.

As the flames tried to consume his vines, he felt his strength draining to maintain them.

Lucky for him, his opponent ran out of power first and the flames vanished.

Focusing on the lifeforms he sensed beyond the elevator, he began his counterattack. Vines lashed out from every direction, their thorns shredding flesh and sending bodies to the floor.

Satisfied that he would face no more opposition, Miguel lowered the vine barrier and stepped out of the elevator. In a grand entry hall beyond the doors, eight bodies lay unmoving on the floor, their once-fine clothes reduced to tatters. Bright light poured in from deeper in the apartment.

Vines crisscrossed the room making him think of the jungle on the necromancer's island. Where did they come from way up here? He was hundreds of feet from anything resembling earth.

The vines don't grow. You summon them directly from Baphomet's hell. When they appear, it's through a magical portal.

No wonder it took so much energy to use them.

"It's safe," Miguel said. "Come out here and tell me if one of these people is the boss."

Old Man joined him and quickly looked over the bodies. "No, Master, he isn't here. Neither is the wizard that attacked us."

"How can you tell?"

"The bodies are all men. Aside from one, I've never heard of another male wizard."

What Miguel knew about wizards, male or female, wouldn't fill a very big book. The only one he'd ever heard spoken of was the necromancer and everyone regarded her as more of a myth than an actual person.

Miguel closed his eyes to better concentrate. His enemies had to be here somewhere.

His awareness wandered the apartment. There were six floors altogether. He went level by level, sensing nothing living as he went. At the top floor he frowned. There was one room he couldn't penetrate. An invisible wall blocked his mind from entering. That seemed a likely place to check.

"Stay here. I think I found them."

"Master—"

"Stay here and protect the Black Eternals. One slave more or less isn't going to make any difference."

Old Man lowered his gaze in submission.

Just beyond the entryway he found a set of steps and began climbing. There were landings at each level which he ignored until he reached the top floor. A door blocked him from moving beyond the landing. This was also the location of the barrier stopping his mental search. Perhaps there were more traps as well.

Moving well back from the landing, Miguel summoned a thick, pointed vine like a spear and crashed it into the door.

The wood exploded in a ball of flames. When the smoke dissipated the entrance was clear. He strode through, trying to look more confident than he felt.

The top floor was a single huge room. All four walls were made of glass and sunlight poured in. His eyes quickly adjusted but the glare made him nauseous. A slender man in a white suit sat behind a desk made of light-colored wood. He had dark skin and a perfectly trimmed goatee. Standing beside him was a woman dressed in a crimson robe, a wand surrounded by flames in her right hand. That would be the wizard.

"So, you're the punk trying to take over my organization," the boss said.

"I dislike the term 'punk,' but otherwise you're correct. And you're the one that sent those gunmen to kill me. Talk doesn't interest me. You have two choices, submit to me or die."

"Are you a wizard like Conryu Koda?" the woman asked.

Miguel didn't know who that was. "I am a hellpriest of Baphomet. I'll have your answer, now."

She pointed the wand at Miguel and opened her mouth.

A vine burst through her open lips and out the back of her skull, killing her instantly.

There was an explosion and a dull pain filled Miguel's chest. The boss had pulled a gun from his desk and fired. The flattened bullet clattered to the floor.

"That hurt." Vines erupted from every direction, wrapping the boss up like a mummy until only his wide, frightened eyes were visible. "I guess I have my answer."

Miguel walked over and stood beside the bound man. Vines wrapped them up and they vanished only to reappear a moment later on the first floor in a large sitting room beyond the entryway. More windows sent sunlight streaming in.

Grimacing, he willed vines to appear and cover every inch of the glass until blessed darkness filled the space. Letting out a sigh of relief, Miguel dropped into one of the couches. The ache in his chest was gone already. When he touched the spot where the bullet hit, the skin felt perfectly smooth. As he thought, normal weapons couldn't hurt him.

But don't assume any gun pointed at you is normal. An above-average wizard could infuse light magic into a bullet and if that hit you, it would do considerable damage.

Miguel appreciated the warning and getting shot hurt badly enough that he was in no hurry to repeat the experience even with a regular bullet.

With a thought, he summoned Old Man who quickly entered the dark living room. "Master, are you well?"

"Fine. And I found our man. Set the Black Eternals on the coffee table. It's time to make plant food."

20

After a great deal of honking and wailing of sirens, Jonny and Diane finally made it to the cordoned-off area around the insurance company's office building. Three armored vehicles formed a semicircle around the entrance. Dozens of cops in uniform were directing people fleeing the building toward a holding area a safe distance away.

Every few seconds another group would come racing out of the building, hands raised, to be guided to safety. Shots rang out, drawing a scream from someone in the distance.

"Sounds like a war zone," Jonny said.

Diane nodded and finally a uniformed officer lifted the yellow tape so she could drive under it.

Halfway through she rolled her window down. "Who's in charge?"

"Captain Rutledge," the officer said. "You can find him in the command trailer."

"Thanks." Diane pulled the rest of the way through and drove slowly to a semi trailer with antennas and a satellite dish sticking out of it. "We need to check in with the captain before we can talk to the survivors."

"Do you know Rutledge?" Jonny asked.

"He's the SWAT commander. We've never spoken, but he has a reputation as a good, if intense, cop."

"Want me to wait here? I don't want to butt into any police business."

"No, you'd better come along. If he sees you poking around, it'll be easier if you've already been introduced. Besides, our work has the blessing of the police commissioner and your base commander, so there shouldn't be any issues."

In Jonny's experience, whenever more than one person was in charge, there were always issues. But this was Diane's show and if she thought it best that he meet the captain, he'd go along.

She parked behind the trailer and they got out. Around front, an officer stood in front of the door. Diane brushed past him, but when Jonny tried to join her the guard shifted to block him.

"No civilians," he said.

"Private Salazar isn't a civilian," Diane said. "I'm working on a joint investigation with the military. Now step aside, we need to speak with Captain Rutledge."

The officer didn't look happy about it, but he did move out of the way.

Jonny followed Diane up the steps and into a long room filled with more computers and screens than he'd ever seen in one place. Uniformed officers manned six stations while a tall, broad-shouldered man sporting a crew cut that wouldn't have drawn a complaint on the base watched a set of monitors. On them were camera views from what Jonny assumed were the

SWAT teams dealing with the creatures that had appeared in the building.

A blast of flames appeared on one of the screens, confirming Jonny's guess.

Diane cleared her throat and Captain Rutledge finally turned to face them. A deep scowl creased his craggy face. "What?"

"Officer Diane Sif reporting in. My new partner and I are investigating the appearance of one of the new creatures. The victim worked in this building. We wanted to speak with any survivors."

"Goodway Insurance?" Rutledge asked.

"Yes, sir," Diane said. "How did you know?"

"Best we can tell that's the epicenter of this outbreak. Unfortunately, before we could secure the building, those things bit a number of other victims, transforming them as well. We don't know how many of the things we're dealing with."

"We're trying to trace the original vector of infection. Our working theory is some sort of drug. I was hoping one of the survivors could give us a line on our victim's dealer. From there, maybe we can figure out what he's dealing."

"Best of luck to you. Stopping the outbreak at the source would save my teams a lot of work. Anyone gives you any shit, you send them to see me."

"Yes, sir."

Rutledge turned back to his screens and they hurried out of the trailer. Once they were away from everyone and on their way to the holding area Jonny said, "He seemed reasonable."

"You sound surprised. Rutledge is in charge of the SWAT operations. Our investigation is on another track. I didn't technically have to speak to him at all. It was out of courtesy, one cop to another and he appreciated it. Besides, these attacks have SWAT working triple time. If anyone wants to put a stop to it, they do."

The survivors had been evacuated to a holding area a quarter mile from the building. Canopies had been raised to offer shade and an officer was handing out bottled water to anyone that wanted one. For the most part, everyone was sitting and staring with a vacant look as if unable to comprehend what had happened.

Jonny understood how they felt. He barely understood what happened when one of those things showed up on his patrol and he was trained to deal with that kind of thing. These poor people were just doing their jobs when all hell broke loose, literally.

"Keep an eye on their reactions when I ask for information. If anyone looks shady, we'll make sure to talk to them."

He nodded. While interrogation wasn't his specialty, the recruits all learned the basics during training. Deep inside, Jonny wondered if Major Evans shouldn't have assigned one of their MPs to this job.

"Ladies and gentlemen," Diane said. "May I have your attention please?"

When everyone had turned her way, she continued. "We're investigating the death of Amelio Lopez who worked at Goodway Insurance. Did anyone know him? Also, we were informed that he may have had a drug habit. Anyone that knows anything about who might have been dealing, please speak up. You won't be in any trouble."

Jonny noticed nothing out of the ordinary as two people, a man in a sweat-stained gray suit and a woman in a torn green blazer and pencil skirt, raised their hands.

Diane waved them over and the four of them moved a little

way away from the gathering. Behind them the occasional crackle of machine gunfire filled the air. Sounded like the SWAT boys were having a time of it in there. Poor bastards.

"What can you tell us?" Diane asked.

"I knew Amelio," the man said. "He was a good guy if a bit high strung. I...I introduced him to his dealer. I haven't used in six months, but back in the day, I had quite a habit. The guy you're looking for is called Gonzo. I don't know his real name. He's about thirty-five, lots of tattoos and piercings, works Third Street near the coffee place. After dark, if you know what I mean."

"That's not right," the woman said. "I saw Amelio getting something from Kevin Green, our IT guy. Two days ago, I accidentally walked in on them in the copy room. Amelio pocketed whatever he had before I could get a good look and hurried out."

The first guy shrugged. "Maybe he switched suppliers. Happens all the time."

"Thank you both very much." Diane jotted down their contact information.

They returned to the car and she switched on the built-in laptop. "Let's see what we can see. Gonzo, here we go. Street-level pusher with a sheet as long as my arm."

Jonny leaned over for a better look. The guy on the screen would have been a nightmare passing through a metal detector. He had more studs in his face than Jonny could count.

"Uh-oh. Gonzo's body was found yesterday." Diane scrolled down further. "Cause of death, murder, heart ripped out and most of his blood missing. Lovely. Now Mr. Green."

"Do you think Amelio's dealer got killed so he went looking for a new hookup?" Jonny asked.

"That's a good theory. Looks like Kevin from IT is clean.

No record and no reports of any run-ins with the law. Might be just a user sharing his stash."

"Who took over for Gonzo?" Jonny asked. "I can't imagine his employer didn't replace him as soon as possible."

Diane frowned and switched back to Gonzo's file. "Looks like he worked for the Alpha Z cartel. Vice isn't my usual beat. If they got their hands on some kind of cursed drug, the sooner we get it off the street, the better. I'll arrange a meeting with someone from vice. Hopefully they can point us in the right direction."

21

As they drove out of the city center and into a residential area, Jonny stifled a yawn. Things had been crazy today and he was starting to feel it. It didn't seem possible that he and Diane had been working together for only a few hours. He glanced at the clock in the dash. Three in the afternoon. How long was this day going to last?

"It was a bit of luck that a detective needed magical advice for a case," Diane said, knocking him out of his trance. "Most of my colleagues are busy burning monsters, so we agreed to swap information."

"What did he need help with?" Jonny asked.

"She. Apparently she thinks magic was involved at her crime scene and she wants me to confirm as well as identify the type. Simple stuff."

Jonny nodded as if he had any real idea what she was talking about. His knowledge of magic was limited to the fact that his two best friends could do it and if you couldn't, it was best to keep your distance.

"This detective knows about the Alpha Z cartel?" he asked.

"Yeah. She's been after them for two years. The crime scene is a suspected cartel drop she's had her eye on for a couple months."

"Okay, and what makes her think magic was involved?" They rounded a corner and he spotted an SUV on the edge of the street with a vine such a dark green it looked black growing out of its hood. The car's engine was clutched at the top of the vine. "Never mind."

Police vans and cars surrounded the SUV and nearby house. Little yellow tags littered the ground and people were busy taking pictures of everything. It looked like a scene out of a cop show mixed with Jack and the Bean Stalk.

Diane parked just outside the crime scene tape and they got out. A woman in dark slacks and a white blouse with a holstered pistol on her right hip and a badge around her neck waved at them from beside the SUV. Jonny pegged her at midthirties though the deep worry lines made her look older.

The women shook hands and the detective said, "I'm glad you could come out. Command said it might be weeks before a department wizard could squeeze me in. You'd think there was no other crime in the city the way they're focusing on this weird monster outbreak. Who's the soldier?"

"Private Salazar and I are working on the monster outbreak as part of a joint military–PD investigation."

"Jonny." He held out his hand and she shook it. The detective's grip was stronger than some men he knew.

"Kate. If you're here, it must be worse than I thought." She waved them over to the SUV. "If you can give me a read on the vine, I'll answer whatever I can about the cartel."

Diane went over and started muttering magic mumbo

jumbo. Jonny knew enough to keep his distance. Instead, he turned to Kate. "Mind if I ask what happened?"

She shrugged. "Looks like a hit gone bad. We collected four bodies and another four survivors fled the scene. We're trying to track them down now. How'd the military get roped into the investigation?"

"We've been killing these things off and on during beach patrol and the research department is trying to figure them out. Your boss and my boss decided to put a team together to share information. I've fought two of these things and you can't kill them with ordinary bullets, only fire and magic."

"I hope I don't run into any then."

Diane turned away from the vine and came to join them.

"What did you find?" Kate asked.

"It's magic alright, the same kind that makes our monsters go, a mixture of dark and earth. Apparently, the spell that creates the monsters isn't the only thing this new magic can do."

"Wait," Jonny said. "If this is a spell and not a cursed drug like we thought, doesn't that imply there's a wizard running around able to use magic you've never heard of?"

"Yes and that's so much worse I don't even like to think about it."

"Cursed drugs?" Kate asked. "This is the first I'm hearing about that. Maybe you should fill me in."

Diane did so and with more candor than their superiors would probably like. When she finished, she said, "Our last victim was a user and then we had an outbreak at his place of work. So, cursed drugs was our guess. Now, I just don't know."

"You think the wizard is using the cartel to distribute this cursed stuff?" Kate asked.

"It's just a theory based on the fact that our victim bought from a dealer named Gonzo who was recently murdered."

"I pulled that one too." Kate grimaced. "Nasty business. If the Alpha Zs are mixed up in this, the one you need to talk to is the local boss, Carlos the Dandy. He's always willing to speak to the cops since we can never get any actual proof he broke the law. He lives in a penthouse apartment in the city center. The building is called The Spire."

Kate gave them the address and Diane thanked her.

As Jonny and Diane made their way back to the car, he asked, "Do we just go knock or do we try for a warrant?"

"Let's knock. If he stays as clean as Kate said, we won't qualify for a warrant anyway."

"Okay. I've got a friend at the Arcane Academy. What me to give her a call and see if she knows anything about this new magic?"

"That would be great. In fact, if I can talk to her, that would be even better."

"I don't think that would be a problem. Maria loves talking about magic." Jonny just hoped she'd speak to him after he set Conryu up.

22

It took all of Maria's willpower not to throw the worthless notebook she'd gotten from Angus across the library. Everything in the stupid thing was speculation. Reading it reminded her of reading fairy tales only they were less believable.

Her last conversation with Conryu hadn't been any more enlightening. He still had no idea how long it would be before the Reaper released him from his current task so he could come home. She really wanted to get into the magic library and talk to the librarian. Surely the ancient spirit would have some insight to the current situation.

Of course, he had lived long after the ancient times when the other demon lords were active in the world. She probably shouldn't get her hopes up.

Her cellphone rang and she pulled it out of her pocket. Since class was over for summer break, Dean Blane had given her the phone back on the off chance an emergency arose. Another emergency that was.

She checked the number and scowled. Jonny. He had a lot of nerve calling her after the stunt he pulled.

Maria hit ignore and tossed her phone on the desk.

Think! Where hadn't she checked? Dean Blane was on the phone all the time with other research facilities and they'd come up as blank as her. Or so they claimed. She wouldn't have put it past them to lie. Old habits and all that.

Her phone rang. Jonny again.

She snatched it up and hit answer. "What?"

"I need your help."

"Ha! You're lucky Conryu didn't feed you to Cerberus after the stunt you pulled. Give me one good reason I should lift a finger to help you."

"We've run into a new kind of magic down here, something none of the wizards have encountered. I thought maybe you could help us figure out what's going on."

Intrigued despite herself Maria said, "Can you give me some details?"

"Hang on, I'm going to put you on speaker. My new partner is Diane Sif, Miami PD wizard. She can explain it better than me."

A female voice said, "So the new magic we're dealing with is a combination of dark and earth magic, which based on everything I've been taught shouldn't be possible. The primary vector seems to be plants, vines specifically. There are also new monsters running around with the same magical signature. They're vulnerable to fire and light magic. We're pretty sure there's at least one wizard using this new magic, but we haven't encountered her yet. Does any of this mean anything to you?"

Maria's excitement grew by the second as Officer Sif explained the situation. This was proof that the new demon lords were making moves here. Not that it was a good thing, but at least they weren't guessing anymore.

"It does," Maria said at last. "Have you two been briefed on the current dark magic emergency?"

"No one said a thing to me," Jonny said.

"Nor me, though the department's lone dark aligned wizard did have a one-on-one chat with the chief. Can you fill us in?"

Maria frowned. Could she just tell them everything of her own volition? Maybe just the basics would be okay. If they were going into battle against someone wielding this strange new magic, they'd need all the intel they could get.

"Alright, but this isn't exactly meant for the general public. As best we can tell, there are eight more hells, each ruled by a lord as powerful as the Reaper."

"Heaven above! Are you serious?" Officer Sif asked.

"Deadly serious. For the past five thousand years, earth has been under the control of the Reaper, but that came to an end a few weeks ago. We've been searching for signs that the other eight are making moves against our world. There's been some circumstantial evidence, but your encounter is the first hard proof. Be careful. It seems much of what we assumed about dark magic isn't the truth. Assume you can run into just about anything."

"How did you learn all this?" Jonny asked.

"Guess."

"Conryu?"

"Yes. He's in Hell right now filling in for the Reaper and learning all he can about the other eight lords. I'll let him know what you've learned."

"Thanks, Maria," Jonny said. "Maybe when this is over the three of us can get together and sort things out."

"He might be willing to let bygones be bygones," Maria said.

"But I'm not. You could have gotten him killed, Jonny. I don't think I'll ever forgive you for that."

She hung up and glared at the phone. Of all the nerve, thinking she'd just overlook what he did. If it wasn't the end of everything they knew, she wouldn't have even answered the phone.

Shoving Jonny to the back of her mind Maria said, "Kai, could I speak to you for a moment?"

A little shiver ran through her when the ninja appeared. "I'm at your service."

"You heard what Jonny said?"

"Yes. You wish me to tell the Chosen?"

"Please. I know you're supposed to watch over me at all times, but Melina and the others can do that for however long it takes you to reach him, right?"

When Kai didn't speak for a few seconds, Maria wondered if she'd refuse, but at last she nodded. "As you wish. I will return as quickly as I can."

Kai vanished and Maria found herself alone again. Whatever was happening in Miami, there was nothing she could do about it. Her vulnerability to dark magic made her a poor choice to go to battle with a dark magic user.

If this turned into a real war, she'd be useless. Maria hated feeling useless.

———

Conryu sat on the Reaper's throne and rubbed the bridge of his nose. He now knew far more than he ever wanted to about the nature of the universe and the altogether nasty beings that populated it. As far as he was concerned, the lessons were over. He just needed the Reaper to get back and set him free from his new job.

He'd never expected to feel sympathy for the Reaper, but if this was the lord of Hell's day-to-day life...

He shook his head. It wasn't an existence he'd choose, unlimited power or not.

At least the black-winged angels weren't worshiping him today. The guards were lined up along the wall, still and silent as statues. They had to be bored as well. There were just enough of them for a football game. If he asked, he had no doubt they'd play.

He grinned at the thought of the gorgeous women chasing each other about the throne room. No doubt the Reaper would be thrilled to have his personal guards playing for Conryu's amusement.

When he sensed Kai approaching Black City anxiety warred with relief for the distraction. Relief won and he summoned her directly to the throne room. She appeared and after an instant of surprise bowed.

"I didn't expect to see you, Kai," Conryu said. "Is everything okay?"

"With Maria, yes. But another matter has come up. One of the demon lords has begun making moves."

"Hold on. Narumi." His teacher appeared a few feet away. "You need to hear this. Go ahead, Kai."

Kai told them about Jonny's phone call and the wizard using strange dark magic through the medium of vines.

When she finished Conryu said, "Sounds like Baphomet, don't you think?"

Narumi nodded. "Very good, Chosen. I wasn't always certain you were paying attention to my lessons. It's good to see I was mistaken. It sounds very much like the work of the Lord of the Cursed Earth. From the sounds of it, his Chosen has already begun building an army of thralls. Spread the word to everyone you can that they need to use light magic infused flames. That combination is the most effective against Baphomet's magic."

Kai bowed. "Yes, teacher. Chosen, do you have any message for Maria?"

Conryu scrubbed his hand across his face. "Just tell her I'll be back as soon as I can and until then to take care of herself. You and the other girls too, Kai."

"Don't worry about us, Chosen. We all await your safe return. I'll begin the journey back now."

"No need." Conryu waved a hand and she was instantly back in the borderlands near Maria. He turned to Narumi. "I hate this. I'd rather fight an army than sit around here waiting."

"So you've told me," Narumi said. "But we all have our parts to play. Don't worry, your turn will come soon enough. And when it does, you mustn't underestimate the power of the other Chosen. Though their magic is vastly different from your own, they will be among the strongest opponents you've ever faced."

Conryu nodded. He recognized that everything she said was true, but that didn't make it a bit easier to accept.

23

When Maria hung up on Jonny his mind was spinning. Conryu filling in for the Reaper was less of a surprise than the idea that there was more than one hell. That little tidbit took everything he thought he knew and turned it upside down. Did it mean that this wizard they were hunting was as powerful as Conryu? He hoped not for everyone's sakes.

At the wheel, Diane was rigid and he could see the whites of her eyes. Her throat worked as she tried to swallow. At least the traffic was light. Given her mental state, he wouldn't have wanted her to have to make any quick moves.

"Hey, you okay?" he asked.

She blinked and shook her head. "Okay might be a stretch. Your friend sounded pretty pissed at you. Could she have been telling us a story?"

"Maria might hate my guts, but she wouldn't make up something like this. Do you want to call in backup?" He hoped she might say yes. Jonny had been feeling a little out of his depth before, but now he was drowning.

"From whom? The whole department is busy fighting monsters. What about the military?"

Jonny shook his head. "A single private on a joint investigation is one thing, but a full mobilization into the city would probably take a presidential order and I doubt we have time to get one. Looks like it's just you and me."

"I'm less optimistic about our chances than I was half an hour ago. Still, maybe Carlos will tell us something useful. If we have a definite target, I can probably get a SWAT team to raid it. There's his building now." Diane pulled off the street and down into an underground parking lot.

The building was a steel-and-glass skyscraper and Jonny wouldn't be able to afford an apartment here if he saved for a hundred years. She parked the patrol car between a pair of luxury cars that together probably cost as much as a tank.

"This is so not my neighborhood." Jonny got out of the car and leaned on the roof.

Diane joined him and shrugged. "I certainly can't live here on a cop's salary. Even a police wizard doesn't make that much extra. Come on. There's a private elevator that goes up to his apartment."

He followed her down a line of fancy cars, including one that looked like it came from the fifties, until they reached an elevator with a monitor beside it. She pressed the call button and took a step back.

A few seconds later the face of a brown-skinned man about forty appeared in the monitor. "What do you want?"

"We'd like a word with Carlos," Diane said. "Is he available?"

"You got a warrant?"

Jonny and Diane shared a look. This wasn't going at all the way Kate said it would.

"No," Diane said. "I was told Carlos was on friendly terms with the police."

"Things change. Now fuck off."

"Wait. Can I at least leave my card in case you change your mind?"

"Drop it on the ground in front of the elevator. Someone will be down to collect it later." The screen when blank.

"Friendly," Jonny said. "I think your friend the detective led us astray."

"Maybe." She set a business card down directly in front of the elevator door. "Let's find somewhere out of sight. I want to see who comes and gets it."

"You think someone actually will?"

She shrugged. "I hope so. If it's someone with an outstanding warrant, I'll have no trouble getting permission to search the apartment."

Diane led him to a shadowy spot across from the elevator. They settled onto the hard ground.

"Is this your first stakeout?" she asked.

"Yeah, I guess it is. Shouldn't we have coffee and donuts or something?"

"You've seen too many movies. Besides, we probably couldn't afford the coffee or donuts in this part of the city."

Jonny grinned. Diane was starting to grow on him. She wasn't exactly his type, but having a wizard cop for a friend couldn't hurt.

———

Miguel opened his eyes when the murmur of voices stopped. He'd been practicing sending his consciousness out of his body to check on the thralls. They were spreading nicely despite losing a few to the police and their allies. He had several hundred now that he could call upon should the need arise.

He'd just finished commanding them to keep their efforts to the poor and run-down sections of the city. Not that he could put it exactly that way. The thralls' intelligence was too limited for such detailed instructions. Instead, he imprinted the image of slums and homeless people on their minds along with the instruction to focus their efforts there. The powers that be generally cared less for the poor than the wealthy. The incident at the insurance office had drawn far too much attention for his liking.

Heaving himself up off the wonderfully comfortable couch, he padded across the carpet and looked down from the second-floor landing. Old Man was just coming back from the door.

"What was that?" Miguel asked.

"A cop. She wanted to talk to Carlos." Old Man looked up at him. "Did you complete your meditation?"

"Yes. What did she want?"

"I don't know. Carlos would talk to the cops whenever they wanted. He liked to show them that he was untouchable. Do you wish me to find out, Master? The woman said she'd leave her card in front of the elevator."

"It might be useful for us to know how far along they are in their investigation. Go get the card while I think about our next move."

Old Man returned to the elevator doors out of sight.

Miguel made his way downstairs, pausing only long enough to check on the Black Eternals. The plants had absorbed several gallons of blood and would soon bud. He needed to get pots and soil so he could plant the new growth.

No need for fresh dirt. Just toss out a few of the plants lying around the apartment.

"I'm no plant expert, but can't putting new plants in a used pot kill them?"

The Black Eternals are magical plants. No fungus is going to kill them. As long as you keep them out of the sun and water them regularly with fresh blood, they'll survive just fine.

That was certainly convenient. Now he just needed to decide what to do about the cop. He couldn't very well let her into the apartment. One look at his greenhouse and she'd go straight for her gun. Maybe if she stayed in the entryway?

He shook his head. The smell of blood would reach her regardless.

They'd have to meet somewhere else. Neutral ground. She might go for that.

The elevator opened and Old Man stepped out. He held a small rectangle of paper out to Miguel. There wasn't much information. A phone number, her department address, as if Miguel was going to go there, and her name, MO Diane Sif.

"What does MO stand for?" he asked.

"Magical officer," Old Man said.

"She's a wizard? That's perfect. I need a wizard to consecrate the temple. I can interrogate her then we can take her to the island to sacrifice." Miguel handed the card back. "Call her and tell her we'd be happy to speak with her at her earliest convenience."

"Here, Master?" Old Man gave the opening to the living room a knowing look.

"Of course, here. She's not going to have a chance to do anything about the greenhouse. Now call her."

"Yes, Master."

Miguel rubbed his hands together. First the Black Eternals got a proper feeding and now the wizard he needed dropped right into his lap. Could his day get any better?

24

On tv, stakeouts always took a long time and allowed the partners to get to know one another. He had barely settled into a reasonably comfortable position on the hard pavement when the elevator doors opened.

Diane rushed to get her phone out and point it at the opening. A rather gaunt, pale-looking man Jonny guessed was around fifty appeared from behind the door.

Diane snapped a picture, he bent, and picked up her card. A moment later he was back in the elevator and on his way up to the penthouse.

"That was quick," Jonny said. "What now?"

"Now we go back to the car and I run that guy's picture against the wanted list. If we get lucky and he has a warrant out on him, we can call in backup and raid the joint."

They stood and Diane led the way back to her squad car. She sounded so optimistic that Jonny hated to rain on her parade. "How do we raid an apartment that has a private elevator controlled from upstairs?"

"The elevator is for convenience and status. Building codes

require a fixed exit in case of power outage or fire. That means we can hit them from the stairs."

Jonny had never really thought about it before but that made sense. Who would want to be on the top floor of a skyscraper without a way down when the power went out? Then his training kicked in. A flight of steps would be really easy for a few guys to defend, especially if they had any kind of defensive position built. Booby traps might be an issue as well.

He didn't point any of this out as neither Diane nor her fellow officers were idiots. They would have all the angles figured out before they made any attempt to assault Carlos's apartment, assuming they could even find evidence enough to justify the move.

They hopped into the car and Diane fired up her computer. When she had the cell phone connected, she ran the picture through the police database. Images flickered across the screen so fast he could hardly distinguish one from the other.

A chime sounded and a mug shot filled the screen. It was the guy only about twenty years younger, Ortega Santos. He'd had several run-ins with the law, but nothing recent. He was suspected of running drugs from the Caribbean, but he'd never been caught.

"Doesn't look good," Jonny said when he finished reading.

"Not for us," Diane agreed. "No way we'll get a warrant with just this. I—"

Her phone rang, cutting her off in midsentence.

"Officer Sif," she said.

Jonny couldn't hear what was said, but Diane's eyes got wide. "Yes, of course. My partner and I are still in the parking garage. We can come up right now. No, it's not a problem. If I got offended every time someone swore at me, I'd need a new job. Okay, we're on our way."

"What was that about?"

"It seems Carlos wasn't happy that Ortega sent us packing. He wants to talk right now."

"Is that safe? Considering what we know about Ortega, maybe we should let someone know what's happening."

"That's not a bad idea. I'll call dispatch before we go."

Jonny got out of the car while she radioed in. When she joined him he asked, "What should I be on the lookout for?"

"Drugs, guns, anything that might give us probable cause. This guy's not an idiot, so I doubt we'll find anything, but then again, stranger things have happened."

She touched his chest and muttered something.

"What was that?" Jonny asked. If she was going to cast a spell on him, he would have appreciated a heads-up first.

"Flying spell. If we're desperate, we can leap out one of the windows. The spell's good for an hour so keep that in mind."

They walked back to the elevator and this time when Diane pressed the button, the door opened without an interview. The inside of the elevator was all polished and perfect. There wasn't even a control panel. Jonny had never ridden in such a clean elevator. Back home there would've been empty beer bottles or a puddle of vomit or something equally nasty in one corner. The winch would have squeaked the whole way up and at least one button would have been broken. This ride was silent and smooth.

A chime rang and the door opened on a luxurious entry room. Jonny had no time to take any of it in as the over-whelming stink of blood nearly made him retch.

Diane managed a single syllable of a spell before a black vine wrapped around her throat.

Jonny went for his pistol, but was quickly wrapped up as well.

When they were both cocooned like a fly waiting for the spider, a bronze-skinned young man stepped into the room with Ortega behind him. The guy was dressed in a fancy black robe marked with strange signs. Jonny had never seen anything quite like it outside of a bad fantasy movie.

The wizard wannabe ignored Jonny and focused on Diane. "If I remove your gag, you won't do something stupid like try and cast a spell, will you?"

Diane managed to shake her head.

"Good. Should you forget, just remember I can crush your voice box or rip your friend's head off with a thought."

The vines retracted enough to allow Diane to speak. "Are you a wizard?"

"I am a hellpriest, the Chosen of Lord Baphomet. You should be honored. Your blood will consecrate the first new temple to my master in thousands of years." He turned to Ortega. "Fetch the car. We need to return to the island immediately."

"Yes, Master." Ortega brushed past them and got in the elevator.

"Where's Carlos?" Diane asked.

"He's feeding the plants. I'll show you." The hellpriest gestured and the vines lifted Jonny and Diane and followed along behind deeper into the apartment.

The smell of blood grew stronger by the second. Crimson lights burst to life.

It was a good thing Jonny's mouth was held shut as he badly wanted to throw up. Bodies of a bunch of men and one woman hung from the ceiling by yet more vines. They'd each had their throats cut and blood was still dripping out onto a pair of plants with shiny black leaves. Each drop was instantly absorbed by the plants.

160

The windows had been fully overgrown by vines. The only light came from tiny cracks at the very edge of the plants.

Jonny had never seen anything like them and he hoped to never see anything like them again. Black plants that fed on blood could only be magical. Their purpose, on the other hand, was a mystery.

"Welcome to my greenhouse," the hellpriest said. "From here, Baphomet's blessing will spread across the entire city and eventually the world. As the master's Chosen, I will rule."

"Who is Baphomet?" Diane asked.

"The ruler of Hell and Lord of the Corrupt Earth. And the new god of this world for all intents and purposes."

"Lord of Hell, you mean the Reaper?"

She groaned in pain as the vines creaked tighter.

"I do not mean that fraud. My master's hell is far greater." The hellpriest cocked his head as if listening to a voice only he could hear. "No, I won't kill her before we return. But I also won't have her insulting the master."

It was becoming painfully clear to Jonny that this guy was absolutely barking mad. He was also insanely powerful. He might even give Conryu a run for his money.

"What's going to happen to my partner?" Diane asked.

Jonny had been wondering the exact same thing though every guess he came up with sucked.

"As you can see, we're nearly out of plant food. I think one more sacrifice will be enough to get the Black Eternals to bud."

That was the worst-case scenario for sure. And he was helpless to do a thing about it.

The elevator bell chimed and Ortega said, "The car is waiting, Master."

The hellpriest looked away and when he did Diane said, "Wind Blade!"

An invisible sword cut away the vines holding Jonny and a moment later the vines covering the window sheared away.

Blinding light and shards of glass filled the air.

Jonny didn't hesitate.

He willed himself skyward.

The flying spell took hold and he rocketed up and out the opening. It pained him to leave Diane behind. His only hope was that these lunatics seemed to want her alive, even if only because they intended to kill her somewhere else.

Jonny swore he'd do everything in his power to rescue her before then.

25

Jonny landed a block from base and started running. He ignored the surprised looks from the people strolling along the sidewalk. Wizards were reasonably common in Miami so seeing someone land on the side of the street couldn't have been that unusual. He could still feel the spell Diane had cast and was certain that if he wished it, he could have flown for a little longer.

Unfortunately, the sky above the base was restricted and protected by a barrier that negated flying magic. The army wizards had been thoroughly pissed when Conryu smashed all their spells last year. Which, Jonny suspected, was exactly why he did it.

He rounded a bend and spotted the main gate. The shadows were long and he doubted fighting a hellpriest, whatever that was, would be any easier after dark. The sooner he got the cavalry underway, the better. He considered going to the police directly, but he had no real standing with them. Major Evans would have better luck getting through to someone in a position to do something about the situation.

He really didn't want to give them a chance to move Diane. Once they did, who knew where she might end up.

At the gate, the same sergeant was on duty. He leaned on the gatehouse and shook his head. "Back again? Misplace your new partner?"

"Something like that. Is Major Evans on base?"

"He hasn't come out this way, so I assume so. Patrols were bad today. Private Stewart got himself killed by one of the new monsters. Starting tomorrow, no more solo patrols." The sergeant lifted the bar and Jonny ducked under.

He didn't know Stewart. Must be First or Third Platoon. "It's getting ugly, Sarge, and I don't think it's going to get better anytime soon."

"Anything I need to know?"

"Probably," Jonny said. "But it'll be my ass if I speak out of turn. Just keep your eyes peeled and your rifle loaded."

"I always do."

Jonny nodded and jogged off. Soldiers were marching in every direction as the day patrols returned and the night patrols got ready to head out. Jonny hated night patrol. Hunting zombies in the dark with a flashlight on your pistol to see by wasn't his idea of fun. More like an unpaid part in a horror movie.

At least there was no one outside Major Evans's office waiting for a meeting. Jonny leapt up the steps and pounded on the door. It opened shortly after that. A pale and haggard Major Evans stared at him for a moment as if he'd forgotten who Jonny was.

The major shook it off a second later. "Trouble?"

"Yeah, serious trouble. My partner—"

Major Evans held up a hand. "Not out here. Come inside."

Jonny couldn't imagine he was worried about security.

They'd lost at least four soldiers to the new monsters. The base needed to know everything and the sooner the better. They sat in the office and Major Evans took a long pull off a cup of coffee.

"I just got off the phone with Private Stewart's parents. We had to burn the body just to be safe and they weren't pleased."

"They'd have been less pleased if he sat up and started attacking people at the funeral. Major, we found the source of the new monsters. As best we can tell they were created by a hellpriest dedicated to a demon lord named Baphomet. His powers seemed to involve the manipulation of vines and other plants."

Major Evans scrubbed a hand down his face. "The wizard's a man?"

"He's not a wizard, sir. He cast no spells, at least not as I understand the term. When Diane, I mean Officer Sif, asked if he was a wizard like Conryu, he got seriously insulted and nearly crushed her to death."

"Priest or wizard, what's the difference? And who's Baphomet? I've never heard of that demon before. And where's your partner?"

"Baphomet is one of the rulers of the other hells. As for the difference between wizards and priests, I couldn't say, sir." Jonny swallowed hard. "Officer Sif has been captured by this hellpriest. He said he plans to sacrifice her to consecrate a new temple. We have to find him and stop him before that."

Major Evans shot him a hard look. "How do you know so much about all this? I haven't even been fully briefed."

"I called a friend at the Arcane Academy and she told me everything Conryu told her about the current situation. It's bad, sir, and I fear it's going to get way worse. Please, sir. Can you mobilize the base to search for her?"

"Not without permission from above. I will contact the Miami PD. They'll have a better idea where to look for her anyway. After that, I have to report this all to my superiors. I'll keep your chat with your friend at the academy out of it."

"I appreciate that, sir. Permission to join the search for Officer Sif?"

"Granted. You're still attached to the joint investigation anyway." Major Evans pulled a pad of paper out of his desk and scribbled something on it. "Here. Get some transport from the motor pool. I'll let them know you're coming."

Jonny stood and saluted. "Thank you, sir."

He hurried out of the office and jogged across the compound to the motor pool. As he went, he dug his phone out and dialed Maria.

Hopefully she'd answer.

Luck was finally on his side and she picked up on the second ring. "What do you want now?"

"I had a run-in with a follower of Baphomet. He calls himself a hellpriest. He's unleashing some kind of monster on Miami. It's not looking good. He also captured my partner and plans to sacrifice her."

There was a moment of silence followed by, "They're called thralls, not that it matters. They're a type of low-level demon. The bodies are controlled by fine vines running all through it. A seed serves as their core. They're weak against fire and light magic, preferably combined."

"Let me guess, you had another chat with Conryu. When's he coming back? We could really use him right now."

"I don't know and neither does he. Dean Blane is keeping the government appraised of everything he tells us. Though we've heard nothing about how bad it is in Miami. I suppose they didn't want to share that little tidbit. Is anything happening anywhere else?"

"Not that I know of. I'm just a private. No one tells me more than what they think I need to know. I'll let the police know about the fire and light combination thing." Jonny took a deep breath. Now for the big ask. "If he comes back, ask him to come to Miami. Not for me, for my partner. There's no reason for her to suffer because of what I did."

"I'll tell him. And take care of yourself. I know Conryu would be upset if you got hurt regardless of what happened."

"Thanks." Jonny hung up and ran into the motor pool. He quickly spotted a motorcycle that looked in decent shape. "Hey, I need that bike."

"You Salazar?" one of the mechanics asked.

Jonny nodded and waved the note Major Evans had written for him.

"Take it. Key's in the ignition and we just filled her up."

"Thanks."

Jonny climbed aboard, turned the key, and kicked it twice. The engine came to life with an anemic whine. If Conryu heard that he'd have a fit. Jonny didn't care as long as it got him where he was going.

26

Miguel snarled as the vines instantly grew over the opening his prisoner cut in them. Shattered glass covered the floor making his footsteps crunch with each stride. He examined the plants with both his eyes and his magical perception. The Black Eternals had wilted a fraction when the light struck them, but the damage didn't look too bad.

The real problem was that his second prisoner had escaped. That meant someone would be coming to try and rescue the sacrifice. It also meant he had to abandon his greenhouse. A pity, but finding a new place to hide them shouldn't be too hard.

He strode back to the entry area where Old Man waited with the woman. He'd thought that with her arms bound she wouldn't be able to control her magic. How wrong he'd been.

"Box up the plants. We're taking them with us."

"Yes, Master." Old Man hurried to carry out his order. "We should hurry. The police will rush here to rescue their comrade."

"If you surrender," the woman said. "You'll get a fair trial. There's no way you can escape now."

Oh how little she knew.

He pointed and vines covered her mouth. Miguel wouldn't make the same mistake twice.

Assuming they were both correct about the soon-to-arrive police, he needed to leave them a gift.

Drawing deeply on his new power, Miguel sent vines into and around the corpses hanging from the ceiling. Using the vines as a conduit, he drew demons from Baphomet's hell and fused them to the corpses. He felt their hunger and rage.

Perfect. He gave them only one command; kill the next group to enter the apartment. Once they completed his task, they'd be free to go on a proper rampage. That should keep the powers that be busy long enough for them to return to the island and consecrate the new temple. Finding a new home for the Black Eternals would have to wait.

Old Man returned with the boxed-up plants. He'd sealed them carefully, so no light touched them. Miguel pointed at the base of the vines holding his prisoner. They thickened into legs. The construct carried her into the elevator ahead of them.

She tried to struggle as they descended to the waiting car. Other than a few muffled grunts, no sound emerged. He had the vine beast climb into the trunk and they set out for the docks.

He'd accomplished a few of his goals and learned a great deal about this city. When he returned in a few days, he'd have thousands more seeds. He'd send dealers all over the country, spreading Baphomet's power everywhere.

Yes, Miguel would show all those who stood in his way the folly of opposing the Chosen of Baphomet.

27

W hen Jonny reached the Miami PD building, the guard at the gate had taken one look at his military ID and waved him through. His destination was the rear of the building where a team was getting ready to load up and rescue Diane. That was the best news Jonny had heard all day.

He swung around to the back of the gleaming steel-and-glass building and found heavily armed men rushing out of an open overhead door. A black armored personnel carrier that was nicer than anything in the base motor pool waited.

Jonny parked his bike and a gray-bearded man dressed in black fatigues covered by a bulletproof vest marched over to him. "You Salazar?"

"Yes, sir." Jonny answered automatically even though this guy wasn't part of his chain of command.

"Captain Deeds." The two men shook hands. "I spoke to your CO. Much obliged for letting us know about our officer."

"Diane saved my life. I intend to return the favor."

"Good man. Unfortunately, I'm going to have to ask you to

wait in the truck when we get there. A new man on the team during a raid is just asking for trouble. I'm sure you're a good soldier, but this is the way it has to be."

Jonny nodded, not at all surprised. "I understand. I don't want to cause you trouble, I just want to see her safe. If the best thing I can do is stay out of the way, I can live with that."

"Captain!" They both turned to see a woman running toward them. It was the detective, Kate, that he and Diane had spoken to earlier.

"We roll out in two minutes, Detective," Captain Deeds said. "Make it quick."

"I heard about your mission. If whoever has Diane isn't a complete idiot, he'll be long gone by the time you arrive. If they're using Alpha Z infrastructure, there's a berth at the dock they sometimes use when they want to arrive unannounced. An informant notified me that a speedboat tied up there not long ago."

"You think that's their escape?" Deeds asked.

"I don't know, but given the timing, I think it's a possibility."

Deeds growled and bared his teeth. "We don't have another team to spare and if you're wrong..."

"I know," Kate said. "I just wanted to tell you in case you came up empty at the apartment."

"Captain," Jonny said. "You said you don't need me. If the detective is willing, I'll go with her to check out the dock. It's better than sitting in the truck."

"I just finished my shift," Kate said. "But I'm happy to put in a little unpaid overtime to help a friend."

"Alright," Deeds said. "You see anything, call it in. Don't try and be heroes."

"Ready, Captain," one of the men called from inside the armored vehicle.

"Good luck, you two." Deeds leapt into the passenger-side seat and the heavy machine roared off.

Jonny turned to Kate. "You and me, I guess. Got a car? Be a little tight if we take my bike."

———

It was nearly dark by the time Jonny and Kate reached the docks. The big warehouses had turned on their sodium lamps and the huge spotlights burned away most of the shadows. Kate parked her unmarked sedan a quarter mile from the cartel's berth and they set out at a walk. She helped herself to a shotgun in the trunk, but Jonny was stuck with his pistol.

Not much of an arsenal, but given the hellpriest's abilities, anything less than powerful magic was apt to be a waste of time.

They walked across the pavement toward the water. There was no sign of activity and Jonny dared hope they got here first. He still hadn't come up with a plan for rescuing Diane when she arrived, assuming she did. His fondest wish was that the SWAT team found her first and got her to safety.

"There's the boat." Kate pointed to a sixty-foot cigarette boat tied up to a rundown-looking wharf.

"The cartel pays for silence," Jonny said. "You'd think they could spring for a little maintenance."

"The wharf looks like that on purpose. Under the rotten wood are steel reinforcements. They want it to look abandoned and unused."

"If that's the case, keeping a hundred-thousand-dollar boat tied up here isn't the best idea."

They found a pile of busted pallets with a good view of the boat and settled down to watch. Aside from the soft lapping of the waves on the pier, the area was silent. That was a relief to be honest. Having a bunch of civilians around wouldn't make this any easier.

"According to my informant, they've never left a boat tied up like this before. The unusual nature of it is why he contacted me in the first place."

"Okay, so how do we stop them when they show up? From what I've seen, guns aren't going to be much use against this guy."

"We don't. If they show up, I'll radio headquarters and they'll contact the coast guard. A coast guard wizard should be able to give this hellpriest a fight."

Jonny mentally slapped his forehead. "I'm an idiot. Even if we can't fight them, I can buy us some time. I'll be right back."

He jumped up and ran over to the boat. There was a tarp and some other junk in the back. Jonny ignored all that and opened up the engine compartment. This thing had twin marine engines bigger than the one in his bike. It could probably get up to a hundred miles an hour. While he wasn't as big an expert as Conryu, he knew enough to find the fuel line.

Jonny pulled his knife and sliced through the lines to both engines. There. No way were they getting out of here now, not without a few hours to get parts and repair the line. That should be enough time for the SWAT team to arrive.

He sprinted back to Kate.

"Are you nuts?" she asked. "What if the kidnappers showed up while you were over there?"

"What if I did nothing and they got away with Diane? It was a calculated risk. The only way they're getting away now is with two new fuel lines."

Kate shook her head but said nothing more. Now it was just a matter of waiting.

28

Cerberus barked and ran after the ball Conryu made to hold Lucifer. They'd been playing fetch in the throne room for a while now and Conryu hoped Lucifer was getting violently ill from all the bouncing. The black-winged angels were keeping well away as sometimes Cerberus didn't stop as fast as he should and ended up slamming into the wall.

Every time it happened Conryu couldn't stop smiling. If anyone saw the ten-foot-tall, half-ton three-headed demon dog acting like a puppy, they probably wouldn't believe it.

Cerberus dropped the ball at his feet and suddenly whined. Conryu's head spun and he felt weak for a moment. When it passed, he knew at once that he was free from the bindings that held him here and that he'd lost the Reaper's power. He found he didn't miss it.

"I have returned," a deep voice from behind him said.

Conryu spun and found the Reaper striding around his throne and down the steps toward him. It was hard to tell since he didn't have a face, but Conryu got the impression Null wasn't in a good mood.

"I take it the others weren't amenable to extending your deal."

"No," the infinitely deep voice said. "Your world will now become another battlefield in our endless competition. You know all that you need to?"

"I think so. From what my friends said we've got an infestation of thralls in Miami and an active temple in Brazil. I'm sure there's more, but that's what I know at the moment. I'm sure there will be more soon enough."

"You can count on it. The others will work hard to destroy your world simply because it was mine for so long. You and the daughters will have your hands full."

"I have one request. Don't make anyone else on earth one of your Chosen. It'll be easier for me if I don't have to argue over who's in charge of the response."

"Very well, but the others will not hesitate to create as many servants as they can."

"Yeah, I figured that. What about the Goddess and the elemental lords? Will they create more Chosen?"

"I cannot say. What they do is beyond my control. Go now and defend my earth."

"You bet. Oh, one last thing. I stuck Lucifer in that black ball. He tried to take my job."

"He will be punished for his arrogance."

Conryu grinned and willed himself back to earth. Whatever the Reaper did to him would no doubt be way worse than anything Conryu could think up.

The Reaper's throne room faded away around Conryu. He expected to instantly appear on the little sand island he used as a safe arrival point. Instead, some other power grabbed him and he found himself completely out of control. Again.

A moment later the feeling vanished and he was floating amidst fluffy white clouds. A feeling of peace and contentment washed over him. In the distance a golden fence with a huge gate was visible. Golden lions guarded it.

"Why did you bring us here?" Prime asked. "I hate this place."

"I didn't. Something grabbed us. Didn't you feel it?"

"I brought you here." A beautiful angel came soaring toward them, her white wings spread and the white robe she wore fluttering in the wind.

"Goddess, this is a surprise. And while it's nice to see you and I don't want to be rude, I really need to get home. Bad things are happening all over the place."

"I am aware. But there are a few things I need to discuss with you. Time has stopped in the mortal realm while you're here. I assume Null told you about our deal regarding your earth and that things were about to change."

"I learned a lot about the other lords and their hells. Sounds like they're already making moves back home."

"Did he also tell you about the ether?"

"Only that it's pure chaos and you guys did something to it so our magic works the way it does."

"It's a bit more complicated than that. The important thing is that with the other lords becoming more active, the spell we created will begin to unravel. Different types of magic will become possible. More men with magical potential will be born. Demons, angels, and other outsiders will be easier to summon. The whole world is going to change and while I hope it doesn't get to the point where Heaven feels the need to directly intervene, that may happen."

Conryu frowned. He'd never imagined either Heaven or Hell getting directly involved with mortal matters. "I thought both sides worked through mortals, like the Chosen. Would you send an army of angels or something?"

"No. We haven't the forces to spare for something like that. We would simply be freer with empowering agents in your world. Right now, you are the only Chosen I have selected. If you get overwhelmed, that may have to change."

"I convinced the Reaper not to make any more Chosen and I'll ask the same of you. Can you imagine the chaos if there were Heavenly Chosen fighting Hell's Chosen in the streets? Normal people wouldn't dare step out of their houses. I'll do my best to keep it under control."

Her smile was radiant. Literally, light came from her perfect white teeth. "I'm pleased to hear your determination. But you will need help. I'm placing a small force of elves at your command. I'll introduce you to their leader."

A golden light appeared and when it vanished a tall figure in silver scale armor with a katana belted at his waist stood on the clouds beside the Goddess. Conryu stared.

It couldn't be. It just couldn't be.

"Dad?" Though the ears were pointed and the eyes golden, everything else was his father's familiar, stern face. "How?"

"When he was struck down," the Goddess said. "I captured your father's soul before it could fuse with Heaven's essence. It would have been a waste to lose such a gifted warrior."

"She offered me a bargain." The voice was the same. There was no denying it. His father lived. Sort of. "Be reborn as an elf and serve in Heaven's army or continue on to my final rest, becoming one with Heaven."

"Your father had the courage to make me a counteroffer," the Goddess said. "He wanted me to make the same arrangement with your mother when her time came. Given that she is as gifted in her own way as he is, that was an easy deal to accept."

Conryu had heard enough. He rushed across the space separating them and hugged his father. "It is so good to see you again."

He got a gentle pat on the back then his father said, "Whatever happens, you must not tell your mother."

Conryu let go and moved back a little. "Why?"

"There are some things mortals are not meant to know and it might affect the choices of her remaining life," the Goddess said.

He nodded. That made sense, though it would be so hard not to tell her. "I won't say anything. How do I call the elves should I need them? Oh, and will warriors of Heaven be okay working with the Daughters of the Reaper? I'll have to be careful if having them on the same battlefield is an issue."

"It will not be," his father said. "When you call, the spell will let us know who your enemies are and only they will feel our blades."

The Goddess held out her hands and resting on them was a silver ring that looked like the same metal as his father's armor. "Put this on. When you need them simply open a Heaven portal, picture your father, and say 'to battle' in Celestial."

Conryu took the ring and slipped it on his right ring finger. It shrank a fraction to fit perfectly.

"Having command of ten elf warriors is a great responsibility," the Goddess said. "Use it wisely."

"I will." Conryu turned to his father and grinned. "Love you, Dad."

The Goddess also taught him two new light magic spells that were of great use against demons, Divine Flames and Divine Barrier. The first was a fusion of fire and light magic and the second a more powerful version of the light magic shield he already knew.

When his lessons were over, the power grabbed him again and he was standing on the sand beach of his lonely island, the moon shining overhead. He took a deep breath of real air and sighed. No stench of brimstone and none of the faint perfume that scented the air of Heaven. It was good to be back.

From the pocket dimension where he hid it, Conryu retrieved the Staff of All Elements and opened the library door. It was time to get to work.

29

The wind from the helicopter's rotors whipped Kelsie's hair in every direction. She followed a step behind her grandmother, ready to steady her should she stumble, but being careful not to show it. Even in her weakened condition, Malice refused anything that smacked of weakness, even the help of her granddaughter. Kelsie was used to it and no longer took offense to the old woman's attitude.

They climbed into the black helicopter and when the heavy door locked in place, the worst of the noise cut off as well. They settled into buttery soft leather seats and buckled their seatbelts.

"Let's go!" Grandmother said.

With a bump and a lurch, they were on their way. Kelsie didn't know much about the necromancer, Shesin Rhavia, that Grandmother sought to speak with. The woman had promised her something that would extend her life in exchange for an elf artifact called the Soul Ring. It was a prized Kincade treasure and Mother hadn't been pleased when Grandmother agreed to trade it away.

Not that Grandmother cared. She did as she pleased and woe to anyone that got in the way.

"What kind of welcome can we expect if we just show up like this?" Kelsie asked.

"If she wants to get paid, an apologetic one. I've been patient thanks to the weird goings-on lately, but I don't have endless reserves of time."

Kelsie had avoided bringing this up since she came home, but it was now or never. "Are you really planning to transform yourself into an undead? Does Mother and the rest of the family know?"

"I am." Grandmother's voice held a hint of hesitance Kelsie had never heard before. "Your mother knows and doesn't approve. She would rather see me in my grave and herself in full control of Kincade Industries. As for the rest of the family, I don't know if she's told anyone, but I certainly haven't. I suppose you don't approve either."

Kelsie considered that then shrugged. "Would it matter if I didn't?"

"No." Grandmother's bitter expression softened as she looked at Kelsie. "I've done things, girl. Horrible things that no one knows about. When I die, I doubt I'll like what's waiting for me. The transformation might not be ideal, but it is better than the alternative."

They flew on in silence. Kelsie tried to imagine what things her grandmother might have done that were worse than the things she knew about and couldn't come up with anything. It must have been truly vile.

Hours passed and finally the pilot said, "We're approaching the island, ma'am. Landing's going to be a problem."

"What problem?" Malice asked. "She has a helipad."

"I'll bring the chopper around and you can see for yourself."

The helicopter slewed around and Kelsie and her grandmother looked out the window. What had once been a fine mansion now looked half demolished. The roof had partly caved in, destroying the helipad.

"I guess this explains why she didn't call," Kelsie said.

"What could have happened here?" her grandmother said more to herself than Kelsie. "Shesin is one of the most powerful dark magic users in the world. No one in their right mind would attack her."

"Clearly someone did," Kelsie said. "Maybe she escaped. Do you want to look around?"

Grandmother favored her with a surprised look. "We've come this far. We might as well. Pilot, see if you can set us down in the clearing to the west of the mansion."

The helicopter swung around and came in for a landing. It was a little rougher than usual, but nothing excessive. When they'd settled, Kelsie opened the door and lowered the stairs. They climbed to the ground and she was immediately struck by the heat and humidity. Kelsie had never spent time in a jungle before and this was nearly overwhelming.

She slapped her neck and came back with the biggest mosquito she'd ever seen. She might not be the strongest wizard in the world, but this was something she could handle. Murmuring an earth magic spell, her skin hardened like stone. She'd like to see a bug bite through that.

"Grandmother, would you like a stone skin spell?"

"I used something a bit more aggressive. Come on, we're wasting time."

Kelsie hurried over to her grandmother's side and they made their careful way across the clearing. Another of the giant mosquitos landed on her grandmother's arm. A black spark zapped it and the bug shriveled up like a raisin.

Well, that was one way to handle them.

It took nearly twenty minutes for them to reached the ruined mansion at her grandmother's pace. When they arrived, Kelsie wasn't sure how they were going to get in. A massive beam had fallen in front of the door and the frame was so twisted it probably wouldn't have opened anyway. In fact, given the shape the place was in, Kelsie didn't know if she wanted to get in at all.

"I don't sense anything alive in there," Kelsie said.

"Shesin isn't alive." Grandmother scowled at the door. "But I can't detect any undead inside either. If she hasn't been destroyed, she would have contacted me. It seems I'm out of luck."

Kelsie tried to think of something reassuring to say, but everything sounded trite. "Maybe we should head back."

Grandmother stared out into the jungle, her head cocked like she could hear something.

"Grandmother?"

"Follow me. There's something out there. I don't think it's Shesin, but it might be something just as valuable."

Kelsie glanced into the jungle and muttered, "Reveal."

There was definitely something out there charged with dark magic. But it felt strange, like no dark magic she'd ever sensed. Granted, her skills weren't even close to Conryu's, but a simple detection spell should have revealed more than it did.

"Are you sure it's safe?" she asked.

Grandmother didn't even slow as she picked her way across the grass towards the edge of the jungle. "I'm dying, girl. Safe isn't a concern for me. If you wish, feel free to remain in the helicopter."

Kelsie desperately wanted to do exactly that, but she couldn't just leave her grandmother to struggle alone through the jungle. She could fall and break a leg as easily as get attacked by some animal or monster.

She trotted over and walked beside her grandmother. Whatever they ran into, they'd face it together.

30

Conryu emerged from the enchanted library directly in front of the Arcane Academy's main building. It was still early evening and he hoped to find Maria in the library. The familiar glass-and-steel building was a welcome sight after the rather grim surroundings in Hell.

As he started up the stairs, he tried to smooth his expression. Ever since learning his father was still alive, sort of, he couldn't stop grinning. But he wasn't allowed to say anything about it, so a stupid smile would only invite questions he didn't want to answer.

"How can you be relieved, Master?" Prime asked. "In Hell you were omnipotent. You could literally change reality to suit your whims. Here, you're just another mortal. A remarkably strong one to be sure, but far from a god."

"Despite our minds being connected," Conryu said. "This is one thing you've never understood about me. I don't want to be a god. I don't even especially want to be a wizard. But a normal life was too much to ask for and now I have to fight a war against eight other hells. You don't have a chapter on that, do you?"

"No, Master. My knowledge is focused on dark magic. The sort you're familiar with. I have no information on how any of the other lords use their power. I learned as much as you did during Narumi's lessons."

Conryu pulled the glass door open. Hopefully Prime learned a little more than he did. Conryu had tuned the lessons out a few times to preserve his sanity.

The open foyer was dark, the chairs and benches empty. And they'd stay that way until fall, when a new batch of students arrived. Despite his dislike for school, he was curious how they planned to update the dark magic syllabus. He didn't envy whoever got stuck with that job.

A weak burst of dark magic heralded Kai's arrival. She took a knee, head bowed. "Welcome home, Chosen."

"How many times have I told you that you don't need to kneel or bow every time we meet? I got enough of that in Hell. How are things here?"

"Maria has been in no danger, but she has also located no other temples. With your permission, I would like to turn her security over to Melina and her squad so I can resume my post as your bodyguard."

"Granted." Conryu held out a hand and helped her to her feet. "Things are going to get bad, Kai. I'm not sure how bad, but bad enough. My guess is what's coming will make Atlantis look like a walk in the park."

"We are with you, Chosen," Kai said. "Whatever you need, just ask."

"I never doubted that. Is Maria in the library?"

"Yes. She's still trying to puzzle out the notebook she received from Professor Angus."

"Ugh! She was that desperate?"

"No stone unturned, I believe she said." Kai bowed and vanished into the borderland.

That sounded like Maria. He jogged down the hall to the library. The door was partway open and light spilled out. Inside she was seated at a desk with a ragged-looking notebook open in front of her. She was about the prettiest thing he'd ever seen in her white robe, hair loose and flowing down her back. If ever there was someone worth fighting for, it was her.

"Hey."

Maria leapt out of her chair and turned to face him. "You're back."

He grinned. "Yup. And am I ever glad to see you."

Conryu stepped into the library and she ran toward him. Five feet away she skidded to a stop, a pained look on her face.

"What?"

"You're shedding dark magic like a dog fresh out of a bath. I can feel it from here. My skin is crawling and my bones ache. I'm afraid to get any closer."

Conryu stared in disbelief. How could this be happening? He felt no different.

He turned to Prime. "Can you tell any difference?"

"No, but I'm a demon. A little bit of background dark magic isn't going to bother me. She, on the other hand, is one of the most sensitive mortals I have ever encountered. Never fear, Master. This is likely an aftereffect from housing the Reaper's power. It will likely fade in time."

"Likely!?" Maria and Conryu said in stereo.

"You should both know by now that when magic is involved, nothing is guaranteed."

Conryu grunted. Wasn't that the truth. "Maybe we should focus on the current situation. Where do we stand?"

"The worst spot in the Alliance is Miami. From the sounds of it they've got thralls crawling all over the place down there and Jonny's in the middle of it."

Conryu grimaced. "You talked to him?"

"Against my better judgement." She brushed her hair back making Conryu wish he could've done it for her. "He sounded stressed the last time we spoke. He was working with a police wizard to investigate the source of the thralls. Last I heard the wizard had been captured by the Chosen of Baphomet and was scheduled to be sacrificed. He requested your help when you returned."

Conryu was still pissed at his friend, but this was hardly the time to hold a grudge. "I guess I should give him a call."

———

The headlights from an approaching car hit Jonny right in the eyes. He and Kate had been watching the cartel speedboat for at least twenty minutes. The anticipation quickly gave way to discomfort and boredom. He couldn't imagine how anyone did one of these for eight-plus hours. They must have had a more comfortable place to watch than they did.

Beside him, Kate tensed and picked up the shotgun that sat across her legs. "This has to be them."

"Do you call in backup now or do we wait and confirm they have Diane?"

"We wait. If this is just some lackey, we don't want to sound the alarm."

Jonny couldn't argue with that.

Finally the lights went off and he could see again. The car

looked like something straight out of the fifties. It had fins on the rear fenders and was about twenty feet long. Where the hell had they found this thing? He didn't know what he expected, maybe a sports car or intimidating SUV. Certainly not a car his father might have worked on in the garage back home.

The driver-side door opened and Ortega climbed out.

"That's them," Jonny said. "Call it in."

"Not yet. We need to make sure they have Diane."

Jonny grumbled under his breath, but knew she was right. A moment later the passenger door opened and the hellpriest got out. The young man looked all around.

Hand on the grip of his pistol, Jonny held his breath. The weapon would do him no good, but the cool metal felt reassuring in his hand.

Finally, the hellpriest strode around to the back of the car and Ortega opened the trunk. Some...thing climbed out. It looked like a pair of legs made of thick vines holding a wrapped-up, Diane-sized bundle. The creature clomped around behind the other two toward the boat. When it moved just right, he caught a glimpse of a pale, terrified face.

Diane's face.

"Call it in," he whispered.

Kate nodded and pulled out her radio. "Detective Sif located, requesting backup. Hostage is being held by a powerful magic user."

A barely audible voice said, "All SWAT teams are currently engaged in heavy fighting. Hold position and wait for further instructions."

Not good. Looked like they were on their own.

"Why won't it start?" the hellpriest demanded.

The group had climbed into the boat and Ortega sat at the

wheel. The starter whined when he turned the key, but nothing happened. That was what happened when you cut the fuel line. Jonny grinned to himself.

"I don't know, Master."

"Well find out!" The hellpriest crossed his arms and glared at Ortega.

Ortega went back to the engine compartment and lifted the cover. Unless he was an idiot, the cut lines would be hard to miss.

"The engine has been damaged, Master."

"Who would dare vandalize a cartel boat?" the hellpriest asked. "Can you fix it?"

Ortega shook his head. "I have neither parts nor tools. But I can call someone. We have a chop shop in the city. One of their mechanics could be able to replace the fuel line."

"I hate delays," the hellpriest said.

Jonny's phone buzzed in his pocket. He scrambled to get it out as the hellpriest looked around.

"What is that noise?"

Jonny jabbed his finger into the answer button.

"Hello?" He barely breathed the question.

"Jonny? Maria said you were having a rough time. What's the situation?"

Thank heaven, it was Conryu and since he was calling that meant he was back in the real world. "I'm in trouble. Can you come here, like, right now?"

"I think the hellpriest figured out we're here," Kate said.

"Dude, are you there?"

A light flashed and a door opened up beside Jonny. He caught a glimpse of the library before Conryu stepped out and the door vanished. The disagreeable black book was floating along at his shoulder and he held a crystal-topped staff in his right hand. If it wasn't for the jeans and t-shirt, he'd make a credible wizard.

Conryu's gaze was focused on the hellpriest rather than Jonny. "I think I've found the source of the problem."

"Yeah, he calls himself a hellpriest," Jonny said. "We're pretty sure he's the source of the thralls."

Further conversation was cut off when a dozen black vines shot toward them out of nowhere.

They hit a white barrier and burned to ash.

"So this is a Chosen of one of the other lords of hell. He's pretty strong." Conryu tapped the ground with his staff and a glowing rune circle appeared. "Stay inside the barrier and you'll be safe."

"He's got a hostage," Jonny said. "Be careful."

"Thanks for the warning." Conryu strode out past the pallets toward the hellpriest.

"That's the male wizard," Kate said. "He knows how to make an entrance."

Jonny just hoped he knew how to take down a hellpriest without getting himself killed in the process.

———

Miguel could only stare when a door appeared out of nowhere and a man stepped out of it. He looked like a biker with a wizard's staff. Whoever he was, he seemed to be on the side of the saboteurs. And if that was the case, Miguel had no compunctions about killing him. Not that he had any even if it wasn't the case.

A dozen vines attacked at his command only to be instantly destroyed by some strange magic. The new arrival spoke for a moment to the vandals then cast another spell. Miguel had no idea what it did, but something about the power sent pins and needles up his spine.

That's light magic, the power of Heaven. Be careful with this one. He is no weakling like the wizard you captured.

The stranger strode toward him with a look of grim determination. It was an expression that said death had arrived. When he looked into his opponent's eyes, Miguel had no doubt that was the truth.

Then Miguel got an idea. "Old Man, if this wizard takes another step, kill the woman."

As he'd hoped, the new arrival stopped. People were remarkably predictable, especially the ones that considered themselves good. As if weakness was a good thing.

"Kai, the woman," the stranger said.

Miguel frowned. What did that mean? What was a Kai?

He dismissed the question as pointless. "You will stand back and let us leave. Failure to comply will result in the prisoner's death."

There were several *thunks* behind him and he felt Old Man and his vine creature die.

He turned in time to see a figure in all black carrying his sacrifice away down the docks.

Before he could summon the vines, he felt heat roaring at his back.

Only his survival instinct allowed him to summon a wall of vines to intercept the blast. Even then the heat seared his skin.

When the attack stopped his vines crumbled to ash.

Flee! You can find another sacrifice.

"I am your Chosen. I'm not afraid of this wizard."

"You should be." The stranger had covered half the distance separating them. "You've had your way here long enough. Tell your master that this world is not his playground and that the people are under my protection."

Miguel snarled at the arrogant man. "And who are you to speak so to a hellpriest of Baphomet?"

"My name is Conryu Koda." The temperature dropped as the wizard spoke. Darkness gathered around him like a shroud. "And I am the Reaper's Chosen."

For the first time since he defeated the necromancer and gained his black robes Miguel knew real fear. Until this moment, he was the one with the power. Even those second-rate wizards that opposed him were nothing in the face of Baphomet's might. But he knew down to the depths of his soul that should he fight this man here and now, he would die.

"We will see one another again." Miguel called the vines and fled.

Conryu held the darkness around him until he was sure the hellpriest wasn't coming back. The guy was younger than he'd expected, not more than a year or two older than Conryu himself. Still, his strength was considerable. That fire spell should have turned him to ash, but it barely destroyed the vines that sprang up to defend him. The way his magic worked was completely alien and would require a completely different way of fighting.

"You let him escape," Prime said. The scholomantic was less upset than confused.

"I didn't let him, I encouraged him with that fear spell and my little speech."

"Why? You could have ended him right now."

"Probably, but there are bystanders here. Not just Jonny and his friend, but I sense people in the nearby warehouses as well as on the container ships down the dock. I couldn't risk them getting caught in the crossfire if I really let go. And holding back wouldn't have gotten the job done."

"Dude, you scared the shit out of me with that trick." Jonny and a woman carrying a shotgun headed his way.

Conryu debated just leaving, but Kai was on her way back and he wanted to see what the hellpriest had hidden in the boat. Whatever problems he had with Jonny were irrelevant compared to figuring out what the hell was going on.

"It was a dark magic fear spell, so yeah. Who's your lady friend?"

"Oh right. Conryu, this is Kate. She's a detective assigned to investigate the cartels." Jonny gave him a brief outline of everything that had happened over the last day or so. "I never would have found this place without her. Kate, this is my friend Conryu."

"The male wizard," Kate said. "I recognize you from the Four Nations Tournament a few years ago. Having you on the team almost seemed like cheating. Pity you didn't get to finish the games."

Conryu shrugged. "Terrorist attacks tend to put a damper on sporting events. Kai's on her way with your friend."

"Colleague," Kate said. "Diane is a police wizard."

"The hellpriest was planning to sacrifice her," Jonny added.

"Charming."

"Chosen." Kai was walking toward them beside Diane who seemed better if limping. "You are unharmed?"

"I'm fine. Good job rescuing the hostage. I wasn't sure how your sword would work on that vine thing since it was made with a different demon lord's magic. Did you have any issues?"

She bowed. "None. My black iron sword cut through both the vines and the thrall with equal ease."

"That's a relief." Conryu turned to Diane. "Are you okay? You look a bit worse for wear."

"Riding in the trunk of a car in the grasp of a demonic plant monster will give you a few bumps and bruises. If you hadn't showed up things might have ended far worse. Thanks." She held out her hand.

Conryu summoned a bit of healing magic and shook her hand. Her eyes widened as the healing spell washed over her. "Better?"

"Much. I haven't felt this good in years."

"What now?" Jonny asked.

"Now I'm going to have a look and see what those two left in the boat. Maybe there's some clue as to where he fled." Conryu walked toward the boat and the others followed him.

He didn't need an audience for his search, but since two of those present were police officers, he couldn't exactly tell them to get lost. Well, technically he could, but he didn't want to get off on the wrong foot with the local authorities.

"If you need nothing else, Chosen, I will return to the borderlands," Kai said.

"I'd like you to stick about, Kai. You might see something I miss."

She bowed and slipped silently along behind the group.

Conryu stepped onto the boat and grimaced down at the still-twitching remains of the man that had held Diane hostage. Even cut into six pieces he refused to die. The only other item of interest was a sealed box resting on the seat.

"I had no idea he was a thrall," Diane said. "He acted like a normal man."

Conryu had no idea what to tell her. What he knew about thralls didn't amount to much.

"Thralls come in several varieties," Prime said. "From mindless brutes right up to so normal you'd never guess they were anything but regular people. Narumi covered this, Master."

Conryu grunted. No doubt she'd covered a bunch of stuff

during one of the many occasions he'd dozed off. "Good job making a note of it then. Should the wrong people in the wrong places get transformed, we could have serious problems. Devising a spell to detect the infestation will need to be at the top of the to-do list."

He leveled the staff at the writhing body parts. The crystal at the tip flashed white and light magic washed over the remains. When it faded nothing remained.

"That takes care of clean up," Conryu said. "Now, what's in the box?"

He patted his pockets. Why did he never have a knife when he needed one?

Kai's sword flashed out twice and the box popped open.

Oh yeah, that was why.

Inside were two potted flowers with black leaves. They each had a pair of large buds that looked about to open. He'd never seen any plant that looked like them.

"He called them Black Eternals," Diane said. "Apparently they feed on blood and produce seeds that can create thralls."

"I'll have to take these back to the academy so they can study them," Conryu said. "Maybe they can figure out some way to change someone back after they become a thrall."

"Unfortunately," Diane said. "These are evidence in the joint investigation Jonny and I are doing. You'll need to leave them with us."

"I'll leave you one," Conryu said.

"While I appreciate you saving my life, I can't let you walk out of here with evidence."

Conryu hardened his voice and put a little darkness into it. "I'll leave you one."

"That's fine, right?" Jonny jumped in, clearly eager to

diffuse the situation. "We're the only ones that know there were two, so as long as we don't mention it, no issue."

"Fine," Diane said. "But I don't like it. Investigations like this shouldn't be handled by amateurs."

Conryu raised his hand and a bubble of darkness formed around the right-hand plant. It rose out of the box and hung beside him. She had a point, but he wouldn't be the one investigating. Most likely that task would fall to Ms. Umbra. If anyone could figure out how a dark magic plant worked, it was her.

"I appreciate the advice," he said. "I'll offer you some in return. Weaklings shouldn't hunt hellpriests. If you get a hint of another one, contact me. A lot fewer people will die that way."

Diane jabbed a finger at him. "Dealing with people like him is my job, not yours."

"No, it isn't. It's mine, at least for the time being. You handle the normal criminals and leave the hellpriests to me. You seem like a good cop and decent person. I'd hate to see your pride get you killed." He turned to Jonny. "So long."

"Yeah, sure. Hey, maybe the next time I get leave we could meet up for pizza at Giovanni's."

"If you can convince Maria, I'll come too. I—"

A sharp squawk on Kate's radio cut the conversation short. That suited Conryu as it was getting a little awkward anyway.

"All available units converge on The Spire. We've got a SWAT team pinned down and a major demonic outbreak. Repeat, all available units converge on The Spire."

"That's Carlos's building," Diane said.

"Sounds like the hellpriest left a surprise behind," Jonny said.

"I'm going ahead," Diane said. "You two join me as fast as you can."

"I'll come with you," Conryu said. "If it's as bad as it sounds, you'll need the help."

Diane looked like she wanted to argue but, in the end, shrugged, cast a flying spell, and took to the air. Conryu paused long enough to put the weird plant in the library before casting a flight spell of his own. Kai had already shifted to the borderland.

Leaving Jonny and Kate behind, he powered into the sky after Diane. With some luck, maybe he could keep anyone else from dying tonight.

32

Conryu only needed a few seconds to catch up with Diane. She seemed like a competent wizard, but lacked the power to even come close to his speed. Not that many people did. Below them, the lights of Miami glittered and flashed. The faint sounds of cars and music reached him even this far in the sky.

Diane glared at him when he came up beside her.

"What's your problem with me anyway?" he asked. "If not for me and Kai, you'd be on your way to an early grave along with Jonny and Kate most likely."

"I told you I appreciated the rescue. Now you should stay out of the way. This is a police matter. We're trained to deal with problems like this. You're a civilian."

Conryu laughed, which, from the frown she wore, did nothing to endear him to her. "I don't know which police academy you attended, but if they covered hellpriests, which didn't even exist a month ago, and demonic plant creatures, then you clearly had better training than I thought. Besides, I doubt your power reading is above eight hundred."

"My power reading is irrelevant as is my training. The point is, you haven't had any training." She started to descend and Conryu followed. Smoke was billowing out from a tall, silver skyscraper. That had to be the target. "Just keep your distance and let me do my job."

He shrugged and slowed enough to let Diane pull ahead. If she wanted to give it a go, far be it for him to stop her.

"That woman clearly has no idea what she's flying into," Prime said.

"No, I fear she doesn't. But some people have to see it for themselves.

As they got closer to the building, the sound of automatic gunfire filled the air. A hole had been blown in the wall and Diane flew through it. Conryu took a moment to surround himself with a shield of light magic along with a stone skin spell.

He flew through the opening and hovered above the battle. A group of men were huddled behind tipped-over couches, their weapons flashing as they put round after round into a group of ten humanoid figures wrapped in thorny vines. The bullets didn't do a thing as far as he could see. One of the members was lying on the floor, blood seeping out of her chest around the fingers of the man trying to staunch the bleeding.

Even from a distance, Conryu could sense the dark magic rolling off them. They felt more like full-fledged demons than thralls. At least they didn't seem capable of using ranged magic. Which explained why the SWAT team was still alive.

Lightning flashed as Diane attacked.

Her spell hit one of the vine creatures dead center and fizzled, its dark magic aura more than strong enough to repel her weak magic.

The demons weren't an immediate threat, but that bleeding woman was near death. She was his first priority.

Conryu dove down and landed beside the wounded woman. He had no time for explanations. Putting a compulsion into his voice he said, "Move aside."

The medic obeyed at once.

The tip of the staff turned white and he whispered, "Touch of the Goddess."

Healing magic flooded into her, sealing her wounds and washing away all the damage. She sat up, her eyes wide. The machine guns continued to clatter beside them. The feet of the couches screeched as the demons pushed closer. At this rate, the trapped officers would be pinned against the back wall.

He had to get them all out of here.

"That spell," the woman said. "I know that spell. There aren't fifty people in the country powerful enough to cast it. You're him, aren't you?"

"You and your team need to get out of here. No offense, but you're in my way."

Diane let loose with another useless lightning blast.

"We can't," the woman said. "If those things get loose in the city…"

"They won't. What's beyond the wall behind us?"

"The sky. That's the exterior wall."

"Perfect." Conryu leveled the staff and loosed a burst of dark magic that vaporized an eight-foot-diameter hole in the wall. He turned to face the demons. "Back!"

Mini tornadoes picked the demons up and smashed them into the far wall.

"All of you out of the building. I'll lower you down."

The SWAT members all stared at him like he'd lost his mind. And having a complete stranger, even one that just saved your life, tell you to jump out of a skyscraper was kind of crazy. Still, he couldn't focus on the demons if he had to worry about protecting them.

"Master," Prime said. "The demons have nearly regained their feet."

"Let's go, guys," the woman said. "We can leave this to Mr. Koda."

"You heard her, out the hole," an older man with a salt-and-pepper beard said.

As the SWAT team ran for the opening he'd blasted, Conryu focused on the realm of air. "Elemental, see them safely to the ground."

The SWAT team out of the way, Conryu turned to the demons. They were ugly things. Dark, twisted vines writhing like snakes hung from their arms and chests. He'd hate to get close enough for them to strike.

Time to see what the elves could do. A swirling, white Heaven portal opened beside him. Conryu pictured his father's new face and said, "To battle."

Elves poured out, their silver armor and matching swords gleaming.

No commands were needed and even his father ignored Conryu as they charged into the demons.

The swords flashed and sliced deeply into the demons' flesh.

The Heaven portal remained open beside Conryu and every second he felt himself weaken a fraction. He'd opened many portals over the last few years, but he'd never kept one open for this long.

Lucky for him, the elves made short work of the demons. The battle was over in less than ten seconds. As they passed back through the portal, his father gave him a single nod.

Conryu let the portal close and blew out a long breath. He'd have to be exceedingly careful how he used that spell. He doubted he could maintain it for more than a minute without serious side effects.

Diane landed beside him. "That. You. How?"

"You're not the only one that's had training. Learned that spell from the Goddess herself. We'd best go downstairs and let everyone know the threat is past."

"Yeah, I guess we should." After a moment of hesitation, she asked, "Why didn't my magic work on them? I burned some of the other thralls with no issue."

"These weren't thralls," Prime said, making Diane jump. "They were true demons bound into the bodies of dead men. Your power was insufficient to penetrate their aura of dark magic. Many demons can negate weak spells automatically. Didn't you learn that in your training?"

"Prime, mind your manners. Sorry about my familiar's attitude."

"No, I'm sorry. In the end, despite my big words, I was the useless one. If you hadn't come, they would have all died while I watched, helpless. Thank you."

Conryu put a hand on her shoulder and waited until she looked into his eyes. "There's a new darkness coming to our world. In the face of that, our differences mean nothing. I will fight them anywhere and everywhere I can. But I'm only one man. It will fall to people like you, everywhere, to stand in the gap and hold. The task is huge, but wizards like us are all that stand between that darkness and the people that can't fight for themselves."

"I'll be ready," she said.

"Good."

They renewed their flight spells and soared up and out of

the building before landing on the ground beside a black armored truck. The SWAT team had removed their helmets and were sitting around waiting.

The woman he'd healed upstairs inched her way toward him as if scared to speak. Not exactly the sort of attitude you'd expect from a SWAT wizard. Her name tag said Cortez.

Conryu smiled in the hopes that she'd relax. "Did you need something, Officer Cortez?"

She licked her lips and took a deep breath. "I read about you, everything I could find, which was surprisingly little."

"If you read Angus's book, don't take it too seriously. He is to serious research what fast food is to fine dining." She cracked a smile as he'd hoped she would. "That said, the man has a remarkable gift for finding obscure information. So, what did you want to know?"

"What's Heather James really like? I was a huge fan of hers when she competed in the Four Nations Tournament. She was your coach, right?"

Of all the things she might have asked, a question about that psycho never crossed his mind. Beautiful and hungry for fame, Heather lacked any morals, at least any Conryu could discern. How could he tell a fan girl that?

"She was…interesting. Heather had a gift for dealing with the media and fame. For me, I prefer to avoid the spotlight as much as possible." He spotted Jonny and Kate running toward them. "If you'll excuse me."

Diane joined him and the two groups met a few yards away from the SWAT truck.

"Are you two okay?" Jonny asked.

"Fine," Conryu said. "The demons have been dealt with and no one died. Tracking down all the other thralls is going to be a far bigger job for all of you. I recommend an aggressive search as they'll continue to spread until every last thrall has been destroyed."

"Us?" Jonny said. "What about you?"

"Miami isn't the only place with a demonic outbreak. Besides, I need to hunt down the hellpriest, so he doesn't repeat this process in some other city. Remember, fire and light magic are their weaknesses. Don't take them on alone. Pair wizards with heavily armed soldiers. If things get really bad, call Maria and she'll let me know. If you'll excuse me."

"Just a sec," Kate said. "If this hellpriest is mixed up with Alpha Z cartel, there's an island where they recruit fishermen to smuggle for them. It's outside Alliance jurisdiction so we can't make a move on it, but you can."

"It's as good a place as any to start looking. Can you give me the coordinates?"

She whipped out her phone and swiped the screen open. A few taps brought up a map and she pointed out an island maybe a hundred and fifty miles off the Florida coast. It couldn't have been ten miles across.

"Thanks." Conryu summoned the library door.

Hopefully he could track down Baphomet's hellpriest and end the threat once and for all. Assuming there wasn't a village full of innocent islanders in the way.

33

"What is this?" Kelsie asked.

She'd been following her grandmother through the jungle for what seemed like hours only to end up standing in front of a vine-covered, partially collapsed stone building. There were strange markings on the exterior wall. On the opposite side of the path lay the bodies of some strange, vaguely ape-looking things that had been torn apart.

"I don't know," Grandmother said. "But it called to me."

Kelsie frowned. She hadn't heard anything. If her grandmother was hearing voices, that couldn't be a good sign. On the other hand, if the voices in her head had actually led her to this place, maybe they weren't just in her head. Whether that was better or worse, time would tell.

"What do we do now?" Kelsie asked.

As if in answer to her question, stone ground on stone as a section of the wall dropped down out of sight. Beyond it, a passage led deeper into the building. A chill ran down Kelsie's spine that had nothing to do with the weather. She was a dark aligned wizard, but whatever was down that passage wasn't just dark, it was evil.

"We should go back," Kelsie said.

"I didn't come all this way just to turn around and go home to die. Whatever's down there, I mean to see it." Grandmother turned her cold eyes on Kelsie. "Will you abandon me now, at the end?"

That wasn't fair, but then very little of what Grandmother did was. "Fine."

She summoned a globe of fire and the pair set out. Fortunately, the floor was smooth and the passage short. Soon enough they emerged in a large, open chamber. There was a raised section with a stone altar. Vines covered every surface.

Kelsie seriously doubted anything good had ever happened in this room.

All around them the vines began to twitch and writhe. From a crack in the floor, more vines emerged, wrapping around each other until they took on a humanoid form that stared at them with glowing red eyes.

"Have you considered my offer?" the vine demon thing asked.

"You offered me power and immortality," Grandmother said.

Kelsie looked from one to the other in confusion. Clearly this thing was the source of the voice her grandmother heard, but she'd said nothing to Kelsie about an offer.

"Those are two things I want very much, but no mention was made of price."

"The price," the demon said. "Is your soul and your eternal service to Baphomet."

Grandmother's wrinkles deepened as she scowled. "I have no desire to be a slave to a demon lord."

"Who spoke of slavery? Service, I said. You increase your own power while increasing Baphomet's influence in the world until eventually you rule over everyone in his name."

"Hmm. I suppose that would be acceptable. Would any soul suffice, or must it be mine?"

Kelsie could hardly believe what she was hearing yet couldn't find the will to speak. Some force kept her rooted in place, her lips sealed shut.

The demon laughed, low and sinister. "Contrary to the beliefs of the ignorant, a soul cannot be taken, only given. It is the one thing you mortals truly own. Only by your own free will can you give it to my master. In any case, what do you care? Your soul is so black it will end up fused with hell and likely used to make a new demon in any case. This way, at least you have a chance of retaining your mind when you're reborn, assuming you please Baphomet."

"Much as I dislike it," Grandmother said. "You make good points. How do we seal the deal?"

"An act of good faith. This temple has long lain dormant. It must be reconsecrated with the blood of a wizard."

Kelsie screamed as vines wrapped around her, carried her to the altar, and bound her in place.

"Your granddaughter's blood will seal your contract with Baphomet. Cut out her heart and place it in the bowl at the head of the altar. Her death will bring this temple fully back to life."

"Grandmother, pl—"

A vine wrapped around Kelsie's mouth, silencing her.

Malice hobbled across the room to the altar. From out of

the floor rose a dagger shaped like a thorn with a hilt like twisted vines.

Malice grabbed the weapon. "It seems you're finally going to be of some use to the family, girl."

Kelsie couldn't even scream as her grandmother approached, dagger raised, ready to cut Kelsie's heart out.

34

Conryu was only a step away from the library door when two black-clad ninjas appeared on either side of him each taking a knee. He didn't recognize them, but then again when only their eyes were visible, it was hard to distinguish one from another.

"Chosen, we have failed," the one on his right said. "Kelsie Kincade is in trouble and we were unable to rescue her. We offer our lives in apology."

He ruthlessly crushed a moment of panic. Ignoring the many people staring at his conversation he said, "In the library, now. Kai, you too."

Kai joined them and he ushered everyone into the enchanted space. With the door closed, time in the real world virtually stopped.

"Now, tell me everything. Starting with your names."

The women bowed and the one on the right said, "My name is Sonada and my companion is Lin. The grandmaster assigned us to watch over your friend. For weeks nothing happened then she went to an island not that far from here with her grandmother. They sought a necromancer named Shesin. The name means nothing to us."

Malice, of course she was involved. Conryu clenched his jaw but immediately forced himself to relax. Getting angry would do no one any good. "I don't know the name either. Please continue."

"They found only a damaged mansion when they arrived," Sonada said. "Shortly after the grandmother led the way into the jungle. They entered a partially ruined flat-topped pyramid covered in vines."

A vine-covered ancient structure screamed temple of Baphomet. "Then what?"

"They went inside and a creature made of vines and dark magic rose out of the floor to speak with them. A deal was made and vines wrapped Kelsie up. We tried to shift back and free her, but a powerful barrier stopped us. As soon as it was clear we couldn't do the job ourselves, we came to you."

Conryu ran a hand through his hair. They had little time. He drew a circle in the air with his staff and said, "I need you to picture the stone building as clearly as you can."

He put his hand on the back of Sonada's head and sent light magic into her mind connecting it to the circle. A moment later a jungle appeared along with the exterior of the temple.

"Now the inside," he said.

"I was picturing the inside," Sonada said.

He frowned and forced more power into the circle.

No change. The barrier that stopped the ninjas from entering must also stop magical spying. Narumi warned him the lords were skilled at hiding their temples. Looked like she was right. That was going to be a problem. If he couldn't either see or picture where he wanted the library to appear, he couldn't open the doors in the temple.

A more direct approach would be necessary.

———

K elsie looked from the tip of the oddly shaped dagger to her grandmother's face. Search as she might, there was no sign of doubt. This was it. After all she'd done to try and help the vicious old woman, her thanks was to be sacrificed on the altar of a demon.

Somehow this fate surprised her less than it should have.

Before the final blow could be struck, an explosion rattled the temple.

Her grandmother staggered away from the altar and ended up on her knees.

Dust billowed in from the passage they'd used and through it strode a familiar figure, staff in hand.

Conryu had come for her.

Fear and resignation gave way to hope. If he had come, she was as good as safe.

The demon rose, gaining mass as more of the vines wrapped around its form. "Who dares desecrate Baphomet's temple?!"

"I've come with the Reaper's greeting." Conryu slammed the butt of his staff on the stone floor and blinding white light filled the room.

The vines holding Kelsie's arms and legs went slack and the next thing she knew she was being carried at a sprint out of the chamber.

When her eyes cleared, she found three black-clad figures surrounding her. They were halfway down the tunnel and rapidly approaching a door floating in midair. Then they were through and safe in Conryu's magical library.

The two ninjas carrying her set her gently on her feet. The third asked, "Are you hurt?"

She knew that voice. "Kai? Where's Conryu?"

"The Chosen is dealing with Baphomet's minions. It was at his command that we rescued you and brought you to safety. Be at ease. No danger will reach you here."

How could she be at ease when Conryu was fighting that demon and her grandmother? He'd tried to warn her to stay away from her family, but she didn't listen. Kelsie imagined she owed her grandmother some sort of loyalty. How foolish.

"Shouldn't you help him?" Kelsie asked. "That demon is dangerous."

"Do you imagine our Chosen would lose to a mere demon?" one of the other ninjas asked.

"We stay behind at his command," Kai said. "With our ability to shift between this realm and Hell negated, we are likely to be more of a burden to him than a help."

When she put it that way, Kelsie couldn't deny her fears seemed overblown. But even so, until she saw Conryu safe and sound with her own eyes, the worry wouldn't go away.

onryu smiled when the light faded. Kai and her fellow ninjas had rescued Kelsie and whisked her to safety. Now he could fight without having to worry about any innocents getting hurt. The vine demon thing lowered its arms and stared at him, the red lights in its eyes burning bright.

Malice staggered to her feet. "Do you know what you've done? Without the girl I'm doomed."

"'The girl' is your own flesh and blood. She stayed with you because she was worried about you and this is how you thank her? You don't deserve a granddaughter like Kelsie."

Vines streaked in only to burn to ash on Conryu's light magic shield. The attack weakened it a fraction, but a moment of concentration repaired the damage. It was so strange using light magic to fight dark magic. Conryu was almost always the one using dark magic in a fight.

"All is not lost," the demon said. "Help me defeat this dog of the Reaper and his heart will serve as well as your granddaughter's."

"Yes, anything," Malice said.

Conryu raised his staff. "Stay close to me, Prime."

The scholomantic pressed tight against Conryu's back. He didn't think there was any chance of mistaking Prime for a piece of Baphomet's corruption, but this spell was new to him and he planned to take no chances.

The crystal glowed white with a crimson core. It was time to test the Divine Flame spell the Goddess taught him.

White flames streaked out around him in a vortex. Light and fire magic combined to scour the stone clean.

He could actually feel the corruption burning away.

His mind became one with the flames, guiding them across every surface so no vines escaped. Malice didn't escape either. Her withered body was consumed in an instant.

The demon held out a little longer, but soon enough the flames devoured it as well.

When the spell finally ended, Conryu fell to his knees and gasped for breath. Even summoning the elves hadn't taken that much out of him.

"Master?" Prime actually sounded worried about him. How novel.

"I'm fine. Just give me a minute."

When his racing heart had calmed and his muscles ceased their trembling, Conryu forced himself to his feet. All around him the stone had been polished by the cleansing fire. The only things that remained were a black ring and the dagger Malice had been holding. The dagger reeked of corruption, but Conryu wasn't certain how best to destroy it. The ring Malice had been wearing was another matter. Maybe Kelsie could tell him what it did.

He pocketed the ring and wrapped the dagger in a light

magic energy field that should contain any lingering remnants of Baphomet's magic.

"Do you sense that, Master?"

Conryu frowned and closed his eyes. Through his link with Prime he felt something. A lingering darkness. Had the flames not done their job?

No, this was something else. Something deeper, under the sacrificial chamber.

"Looks like we're not done here after all."

"You need to rest, Master. If whatever remains attacks you in your current condition, I fear you won't survive."

"No argument. I need to check on Kelsie and Kai. A couple hours' rest should set me to rights."

"Take a day. The temple is going nowhere."

"The temple isn't, but whatever's down there might find some way to flee if I give it too long to recover. Then I'll have to hunt it down all over again."

Conryu left the temple and pointed his staff. The library door appeared and he pushed it open.

He'd barely taken a step inside when Kelsie nearly tackled him to the floor. She squeezed him tight and cried against his chest. He looked over her head at Kai. "Are you all okay?"

"Yes, Chosen. Your distraction worked perfectly."

Conryu waited until Kelsie stopped sniffling and said, "I couldn't save Malice. I'm sorry."

She looked up at him. "She was going to kill me and use my blood to consecrate this temple to a demon lord. And before that who even knows what she planned to do to me to pay the necromancer."

Conryu brushed her tears away then frowned. "Did Malice know about the temple all along? When you left after graduation, the other demon lords hadn't even made their move yet."

"No, now that you mention it, Grandmother originally planned to make a deal with the necromancer that lived on this island. She said she'd trade the Soul Ring for the secret to becoming undead. When we arrived, it was like she heard a voice that led her to the temple."

That made more sense. Conryu pulled the ring out of his pocket and held it out to Kelsie. "Is this the Soul Ring?"

"Yes. It's an elf artifact, one of the Kincade family treasures. Mother was furious Grandmother planned to trade it away."

"What does it do?"

Kelsie shrugged. "You think anyone told me?"

"Well, if it belongs to your family, you should be the one to return it." He held the ring out to her again.

Kelsie made no move to take the ring. "No, you keep it. Whatever it does, far better for everyone if you have it rather than my mother. Heaven only knows what sort of mischief she could get up to with an elf artifact."

Conryu couldn't argue with that. "Alright, I'll hold on to it for you. If you decide you want it back, just let me know."

"Thanks." She hugged him again.

"What now, Chosen?" Kai asked.

"I need to rest, then I'm going back in. Some darkness still lingers beneath the temple. It won't be safe until I deal with that as well."

"I will join you," Kai said in a tone that made it clear refusing wasn't an option.

"We will come as well," Sonada said.

"No. Kai, you will come with me. You two will remain outside the temple just in case anything tries to get away. Nothing, and I mean nothing that comes out of that temple leaves alive. Kelsie, if you don't mind, I'd feel better if you stayed in the library where it's safe."

Kelsie nodded eagerly. "I can do that."

Sonada and Lin had their gazes focused on the floor.

"You do not trust us after our failure," Sonada said. "I understand. We will do our best to earn back your faith."

At Conryu's mental command a couch appeared along with four chairs. He dropped onto the couch and slung his feet up. "That's not it at all. You both did the best you could under the circumstances. I really do need someone to stay outside and make sure nothing escapes. I can't even imagine what sort of horrors might be lurking in the basement of that temple. In fact, you should get in position now. Time virtually stops while we're in the library, but a lot of rules are changing and I don't want to get taken by surprise."

They bowed and slipped out the door.

When they'd gone Kai said, "You should give them some sort of punishment. They'll feel better if you at least chastise them."

"Sonada and Lin did the best they could." Conryu closed his eyes. "I can't yell at them for that. You should prepare yourself as well. When we go in there, things could get messy."

"I will be ready, Chosen."

Of that, Conryu had no doubt.

———

Miguel paced around, snarling at his thralls and generally venting his terrible mood. He still couldn't believe he'd been forced to flee from the Reaper's Chosen. His new powers had made him so confident that no one could defeat him. And yet that man had sent him fleeing like a boy before an angry father.

But he would pay. Oh, yes. Miguel would make him pay for

the embarrassment a thousand times over. His new temple was nearly complete and once he found another wizard to sacrifice, he would consecrate it to Baphomet. Then he would truly be a priest and doubtless his power would increase further.

You must flee!

The voice's sudden appearance and petrified tone stopped Miguel in his tracks. "Flee? What do you mean? The temple is nearly complete."

It doesn't matter. The Reaper's Chosen has found the temple where you gained your powers. I will try to defeat him, but hold out little hope. Once the main temple is purified, you will be on your own.

Panic raced through Miguel. Alone? Without the voice, how would he learn to better use his abilities? Who would guide him in his service to Baphomet?

Wait, wasn't the voice Baphomet? How could the demon lord lose to a mere human wizard?

I am only Baphomet's agent on this planet. He sent me here to guide his new Chosen when the time came. I believed the temple well enough hidden to escape notice, but I was wrong. Once I have been destroyed, you will be our master's only hope. Take the Black Eternals and flee. Find a hidden place and build your power. Draw no attention until you're ready to strike. Hur—

"Are you there? Where should I go? Speak to me!"

But the voice was gone. Defeated by the Reaper's Chosen. And Miguel would end up the same way unless he hid. Scrambling away from the construction site, he rushed into the hut where he kept the remaining Black Eternals. Collecting his last three plants, he summoned the vines and fled the island.

He knew not where he would end up. But for now, survival was all that mattered.

Conryu and Kai stood in the altar chamber and looked all around. They'd been searching for the better part of an hour and still found no sign of an access point for the lower levels. When asked, Prime insisted the darkness was still below them and Conryu sensed it himself when they linked their senses. If there were chambers below, there had to be a way to get to them.

"Should we search the walls again?" Kai asked.

"No, if there was a passage there one of us would have found it. Maybe the easiest way to do this is to make my own opening. Prime, where is the exact center of the darkness?"

Prime flew over to a spot about twenty feet in front of the altar. "Right here, Master, though I am uncertain exactly how far down."

"That's good enough. Kai, move back."

When she'd eased a few paces away, Conryu charged the staff with earth magic and slammed the butt end down on the stone floor. A tremor ran through the temple and cracks formed in the floor.

He leapt back as the floor caved in and huge chunks fell down out of sight. A pit formed until half the temple floor had fallen in.

Massive vines shot up, trying to wrap around Prime who had flown in for a closer look.

Kai leapt across the opening, sword slashing. She landed safely on the other side of the pit and Prime flew over beside Conryu.

"Did I not say be careful?"

"Sorry, Master. I thought I was high enough to evade capture."

"Did you see anything beside the vines?"

"The tunnel continues down beyond them, but I could make out little beyond that."

The only way they were getting through was if he burned the vines out of the way. Summoning the white flames, Conryu sent them roaring down into the pit.

Blackened vines crashed up, thrashing like living things as the flames burned them down to nothing.

When they were gone, he eased over and peeked over the lip of the pit. The stone glowed orange from the heat, but nothing remained of the vines. He cast a flying spell on himself and Kai. When they were floating over the pit he added a light magic barrier.

With the group as protected as he could make them, Conryu willed them down into the pit.

Happily, it didn't descend as deep as he'd first feared. They landed about twenty yards down in another chamber about the same size as the one above. At the heart of it was a black sphere about the size of a bowling ball. The surface looked slimy, like it was covered in oil. Just looking at it made Conryu slightly sick to his stomach.

"A demonic core," Prime said. "This is the heart of the temple and likely the heart of the vine demon from upstairs."

"Okay, so how do I destroy it?"

"You need to hit it with enough light magic to neutralize the dark. It looks pretty dense, so it won't be easy."

"Nothing ever is." Conryu leveled his staff.

Before he could summon the Divine Flames Kai said, "Chosen, something is coming."

He glanced back. Scores of vines were crawling towards them like a carpet of snakes. He had to focus all his power on the core. "Keep them off me, Kai. I'll be as fast as I can."

"My life for yours, Chosen."

"Thanks, but I'd prefer we both get out of this alive."

White flames erupted from the staff and pounded the core.

Once again Conryu felt his mind connected to the fire as it fought to purify the corruption. Through that link he sensed the demon's awareness as the flames slowly destroyed it.

It railed and fought. Behind him Conryu was vaguely aware of Kai slicing through any vine that got close.

Layer by layer the core shrank.

Stop! I beg you. Let me live and Baphomet will reward you with power greater than anything the Reaper has offered.

He ignored the demon's wheedling and pushed harder. The core was burned down to little more than a golf ball when it finally shattered. The tiny pieces of darkness were quickly consumed.

Conryu released the spell and leaned hard on his staff. It was done.

A soft moan drew his attention. He turned to find Kai lying on her back. Dozens of wounds covered her body. Though none of them looked serious, they had to be painful.

A sweep of the staff flooded her with light magic. The cuts vanished in an instant. "Better?"

"Much, thank you, Chosen."

Kai hastened to rise, but he rested a hand on her shoulder. "Take your time. Prime, what's our status?"

"I sense no more corruption, Master. The temple has been fully purified."

Thank goodness for that. Conryu seriously doubted he had strength enough for another burst of Divine Flames.

He pointed and the library door appeared. Time for a nice long rest. They'd certainly earned it.

As he and Kai leaned on each other and limped across the threshold into the library, Prime said, "Master, the hellpriest."

"Shit, I forgot all about him. Sonada, Lin, I've got a mission for you two."

The ninja pair appeared. "How may we serve?"

"There's an island not that far east of here. I want you to scout it out. Confirm the hellpriest's presence and return here. Under no circumstances are you to attack on your own. Understand?"

"As you command." They vanished again.

From behind them Kelsie said, "Are you two okay? You look awful."

"I've been better," Conryu said. "But at least we've dealt with this temple. I really hope the one in Brazil isn't this tough."

Lin and Sonada appeared only seconds later. Sonada said, "We found an island crawling with thralls and there was a nearly complete structure that looked very much like a wooden version of this temple, but no hellpriest."

"He must have fled." Conryu wanted to punch something.

"You did all you could, Chosen," Kai said. "Let us rest. The hunt can resume tomorrow."

"Good call, Kai. Sonada, you and Lin keep watch over that island. If anyone with a powerful dark aura shows up, come find me."

They bowed and disappeared.

Conryu stepped into the library and closed the door. Time to return to the academy. Maybe it had been long enough that he could finally give Maria a hug. Heaven knew he needed one.

EPILOGUE

Conryu strode down the sidewalk toward Giovani's Pizza Parlor. After nearly a week of searching, he'd found no sign of the hellpriest. Even worse, when he went to the temple Maria found in Brazil, the demon was gone and no corruption remained in the temple. He assumed the followers of Abaddon had learned of his victory over Baphomet and found a new hiding place.

It was a setback, but what could he do? They'd pop up again somewhere and when they did, he'd be ready.

On a less pleasant note, he still couldn't get close to Maria. Whatever darkness he'd absorbed in Hell still lingered. He had to keep a good four feet from her at all times lest she start to hurt. And he would never do anything to hurt Maria. Though being unable to touch certainly hurt them both a great deal.

That problem would sort itself out eventually. He hoped anyway. Having to live the rest of his life like this wasn't appealing. Speaking of Maria, her father had invited him to some official meeting at the Department of Magic in Sentinel City. He'd given no hint what it was about during their short telephone conversation, but whenever Mr. Kane invited him to an official meeting, nothing good ever came out of it.

But that wasn't until this afternoon. Now it was time to have lunch and keep a promise. He ducked into an empty alley two blocks from the pizzeria, summoned the staff, and pointed at a spot free of litter. A dark circle appeared and he said, "Dark Lady."

A cylinder of darkness rose out of the circle and when it vanished, she stood there in the biker outfit he'd made for her. The denim shorts, cut-off top, and thigh-high boots looked just as good on her in the real world as they did in Hell. She also had bat wings, horns, and a tail. Since he didn't want to give Mr. Giovani a heart attack, a more human appearance would be necessary.

"Master." She looked all around as if expecting an attack at any moment. "Is all well?"

"For the moment. I've got a few hours to kill before a meeting and thought I might keep my promise."

She stared at him with her red eyes then smiled. "Our date! I didn't think you really meant it."

"I always keep my word. Besides, things have been kind of stressful lately. A few hours with a friend will be a nice break."

Her smile was bright enough to light up the sky. Only the needle-sharp eye teeth spoiled the effect. "Do you know you're the first person, mortal or demon, that has called me his friend? I quite like it."

"I guess I'll never understand demons. If you could get rid of the wings, tail, horns, and glowing eyes, we'll go have some of the best pizza in the world."

As her body shifted into a fully human form, she licked her red lips. "I've never had pizza. In fact I'm not sure I've ever had a proper meal of any sort. It's not like I need to eat."

They left the alley and made the short walk to Giovanni's. Everyone they passed stared at the Dark Lady. Not that he could blame them. Not only was she beautiful, but there was also something about her magic that made people desire her. It didn't affect Conryu since he was her master.

Speaking of which, before opening the door he said, "Best call me by my name while we're around other people."

She took his hand and smiled again. "Calling my master by his given name. Yet another thing I've never done. This is turning into a day of firsts. Shall we, Conryu?"

He smiled back. How was it that the most normal thing he'd done in months was have lunch with a demon?

A delicious meal and two hours of idle conversation passed quickly, then it was time to go to the department for his meeting. Whatever happened there he was glad he got to keep his promise. The Dark Lady only pouted a little when he sent her back and even that expression was adorable on her.

It was a ways to the department building so he took to the air. A brief flight saw him landing in the parking lot of a tall, black building with a pentagram on the front. Not the most welcoming structure in the city.

The automatic doors opened for him and he made his way to a free receptionist. The woman gave him a bored look before her eyes widened. "Mr. Koda. The chief is waiting for you in the meeting room upstairs. Top floor, second door on your left."

"Thanks."

He went to the nearby bank of elevators and rode the nearest one to the top floor. He knocked on the pale wood door and Mr. Kane said, "Come in."

Conryu pushed the door open and froze. Four huge televisions hung on the wall, each with a face centered in it. The only face he recognized was Jemma, the head of the Kingdom of the Isles Ministry of Magic. Maria, her mother, Ms. Umbra, Jonny, and two other women he didn't know sat around a rectangular table with Mr. Kane at the head.

"What's all this?" Conryu asked.

"The headquarters of the Department of Infernal Investigations, temporary of course. We're getting something better set up in Central as we speak. Your mother is overseeing the work. We've formed a working group with the departments of magic in the other Alliance members to look into anything related to the newly revealed demon lords."

"You got this set up in a hurry," Conryu said. "Impressive."

"The four governments have promised us significant resources. The events in Miami convinced them of the seriousness of the situation. I won't mince words," Mr. Kane said. "We want you onboard, officially."

Conryu considered the offer for a moment, but only a moment. "No. I appreciate the offer, but I can't join your group. I'll be happy to work with you when our tasks overlap, but I can't be bound by bureaucrats. They might take me to places you have no sway. If I'm an official member, that will cause you problems you don't need. Any time you need extra firepower, Maria can get in touch with me."

Mr. Kane stood. "We can't just let you run around doing whatever you want. There are rules about this sort of thing."

"Those are your rules," Conryu said. "I answer to higher powers and if I can't do what I have to, they will. Do you understand? If I fail, Heaven and Hell will build their own teams and I assure you they'll have no interest in your rules. It'll be chaos."

Mr. Kane sat back down and ran his hands over his bald head. "You're putting me in a bad spot, son."

"No, I'm putting you in a great spot. Whenever something goes wrong and your superiors want someone to blame, tell them it's my fault. Koda the loose cannon did it again. I assure you, the opinions of politicians don't concern me in the least. If there's nothing else, I need to go."

He turned on his heel and marched out. It wasn't that he thought setting up a group to investigate the new cults was a bad idea, in fact it was a great idea. But having seen the power of a hellpriest and the guardian demons, he feared bringing anyone in the room into battle with him would be signing their death warrant.

Conryu couldn't live with that. He could barely stand taking Kai and the other ninjas into battle. Every moment he feared one of them might get herself killed. Knowing a decent afterlife in the Reaper's court awaited them helped a little, but only a little.

"Conryu, wait." He turned to find Maria hurrying after him. She stopped a safe distance away. "Are you really going to walk away from this?"

"I have to. I'm not sure how to say this in a way that won't sound offensive or condescending, but none of you would last a minute against a hellpriest. Even Ms. Umbra would be hard pressed to go toe to toe with one. Fighting on my own means I don't have to hold back. I don't have to worry about the people I care about getting hurt.

"What about us worrying about you?" Maria took a step closer, winced, and moved back. That little retreat hurt Conryu worse than any spell ever could.

"I don't know what to say. All I am sure of is what will happen if I can't hold back the tide of evil coming toward us. I left Melina and her squad watching over you. If for whatever reason you can't reach me on the phone or with the coin I gave you, tell her what you need and she'll find me."

She still looked so uncertain it tore at him.

Conryu forced a smile. "It's not like I'm going to be stuck in Hell again. I'm literally just a portal away any time you need me."

"Please, be careful."

He wanted to hold her so bad it hurt. "I will."

Conryu summoned the library door and stepped inside before his will broke. He didn't know what was going to be harder, fighting the battles he knew were coming or being away from Maria.

He certainly knew which one sucked the worst.

AUTHOR NOTE

I hope you enjoyed Conryu's latest adventure. It was a lot of fun to write. I'm sure there will be more battles with the demon lords and their minions down the road.

Until then, thanks for reading,

James

The Rogue Star Series:

Children of Darkness

Children of the Void

Children of Junk

Rogue Star Omnibus Vol. 1

Children of the Black Ship

ABOUT THE AUTHOR

James E. Wisher is a writer of science fiction and fantasy novels. He's been writing since high school and reading everything he could get his hands on for as long as he can remember.

To learn more:
www.jamesewisher.com
james@jamesewisher.com